FALL OF THE TAMER

FALL OF THE TAMER

Matthew Getzfred

authorHOUSE®

AuthorHouse™ LLC
1663 Liberty Drive
Bloomington, IN 47403
www.authorhouse.com
Phone: 1-800-839-8640

Published by AuthorHouse 06/12/2014

ISBN: 978-1-4969-1963-2 (sc)
ISBN: 978-1-4969-1962-5 (e)

Library of Congress Control Number: 2014910757

To Lane

Words will never be able to express my gratitude for always lighting my way and keeping me on the right path.

I

Tagori took a deep breath. He had three targets set up—one to his right, one in front of him, and the third directly behind him—each hanging from the branches of the trees that surrounded him in the forest. He pulled back the first arrow, keeping it pointed at the ground. He steadied his breathing and cleared his mind, focusing on the current task. Quickly he brought the arrow up and loosed it, turning before it impacted its target. He spun around, grabbing an arrow and stringing it quickly as he turned and fired it at the second target. Just as quickly, he grabbed his third arrow and fired it at the target that was now to his left. He watched as the arrow flew toward the direct center of the target and was intercepted by the neck of a deer. The creature fell in a heap.

Tagori pushed his curly hair out of his eyes as he sighed, taking time to process what had happened. It took him little more than a moment to reluctantly move the beast onto his thin but strong shoulders. Awkwardly carrying both the deer and his bow, Tagori made his way to Norico, the city that had been his home his entire life, leaving the arrows in the brush where they had landed.

The houses in the town were only a few rooms big, if they were even divided into rooms at all. Tagori took the deer to his home first, hoping that his brother or father would be home to help him. Unfortunately, his house was devoid of life when he entered.

"Why am I always home alone?" Tagori asked himself.

Tagori was a boy of sixteen, though he still acted like a child at times. He tried to remind people that his birthday was quickly approaching.

"You sure you're alone, Tag?" Roz said from somewhere behind Tagori.

Startled, Tagori turned to see where the sound had come from. His brother, Roz, had snuck up behind him. Roz was almost exactly nine months older than Tagori.

"What happened to the deer?" Roz asked.

"Accidental causality during target practice. Any idea if Dad is in the shop?" Tagori asked. Their father, Treth, was a butcher in town.

"I'm not sure," Roz said. "I just arrived myself. Let's take it to him."

"Hold on. Shouldn't you be working?" Tagori asked.

"Cerrum let me off early," Roz said.

Roz had always been a secretive person, talking little about what he did. Although Cerrum was known to be Roz's boss, Cerrum was not known throughout the village.

Roz took the unfortunate creature to the butcher as Tagori went to make a few arrows to replace the ones he had broken. As soon as he was done with this task, he joined his brother and father. He sat in a corner reading and listening to their conversation, as his stomach would not allow him to assist them. It was his aversion to gore that prevented him from perusing his father's profession.

Their father was a tall man, though this was according to Tagori and Roz. In actuality, the man stood hardly six feet, and that was with some generous leeway. Though not overweight by any means, their father did have some girth to him.

"You two are leaving town soon?" Treth said.

"Yes, I thought I would take Tag to find an occupation," Roz said.

"Where do you plan to go?"

"Areno, Arenret … maybe even as far as Kyata."

"Trying to keep him along the coast?"

"It will feel just like home, or so I figure. You like the river, don't you, Tag?"

"I do. I would like to take a trip up to its source sometime," Tagori answered.

"That's too far north, though," Roz said.

"In any case, you come back and let me know how things are going," Treth interjected.

"You know we will, Dad."

"I never know how much I need to remind you. I can't believe I raised two boys with completely empty heads," their father joked.

"At least we know where we get it from!" Tagori retorted.

"Is that right?" Treth questioned. "I guess it had to come from somewhere."

Together they closed the shop and headed upstairs to cook something in the private kitchen, as it was better equipped and simply more convenient than the one at their home. After eating this meal, made partially from the deer, they returned to their home on the edge of town.

Tagori went to his room and saw some sort of oblong ball on his bed. It was as large as his head. He quickly scanned his room, looking for anyone who might still be there. Nothing. How did this ball of what seemed to be ivory end up on his bed? After a few minutes of fruitless pondering, he gave up, wanting above all else to get some sleep. He placed the object in the bottom of his wardrobe and quickly fell asleep.

A fortnight passed, and Tagori kept the object hidden away in his wardrobe. Something like that must have been worth quite a bit of money. He would attempt to sell it if he needed money.

The night before his birthday, he heard something rustling in his wardrobe. He hesitantly opened the door to see the ivory ball trembling. Confused, he touched it, feeling a warmth radiate from inside. The ivory cracked, creating fine lines along the surface. Something poked out from one side of the ball. It then continually poked in and out, causing the hole it created to grow larger. It didn't take long for the head of some small creature to emerge. The creature appeared to be some sort of large lizard. It spread its small, veiny wings with flourish.

Wings? This creature could only be a dragon, something long thought to be extinct. He reached out slowly to touch it. The creature was no longer than his forearm. White-yellow scales adorned the body. Tagori knew that he needed to keep this creature hidden away. If anyone saw him with this, he didn't know what its fate would be.

Over the following months, Tagori fed the creature and watched it grow. The rate at which it grew was amazing. After the first month, it was as tall as Tagori's waist. The following month, it could stand shoulder-to-shoulder with him, at which time he moved it to the forest off the south end of the island. During this time, its scales changed from yellow to green. Horns grew straight back on its head, giving it a triangular shape. The wings had grown in size as well, though it was hard to tell when they were kept at the dragon's side. A sharp point tipped the central joint of the wing. The claws on the dragon's toes had grown as well, giving a startling contrast to the tiny nubs they had been. Its tail had grown a row of spines along the top, running the entire length of the tail to the tip.

"You deserve a name, don't you?" Tagori said after the beast had been living in the forest for only a few days.

The dragon looked happily at Tagori.

"What are dragons named?" Tagori asked rhetorically.

The dragon's light green scales reminded Tagori of a ring his mother used to wear, a simple copper band with a small colored piece of glass meant to look like a gem.

With the gem on his mind, Tagori slowly spoke, his mind elsewhere. "Emrila."

The dragon purred, bringing his mind back to the present.

"Do you want that to be your name?" Tagori asked it.

The dragon put its forehead up to Tagori's. A surge of electricity shot through Tagori's body, and though it didn't hurt, it did make his limbs numb. Looking at his arms, he saw thick black lines run the length, beginning between his middle two fingers and traveling up past his elbow and up the sleeve of his shirt. As soon as feeling returned to his arms, he heard a voice.

"It's a fine name," the feminine voice said.

"Who …?" Tagori said, looking around. The black lines vanished from his arms.

"It's me, Emrila," she said.

"You can speak?"

"Only through your mind. Think and you shall speak to me as well."

"Why me, though?"

"That mark on your arm shows the bond between us."

This mark? he thought, though without any intention of speaking with the dragon. As he looked at his arm, the marks returned.

"In the town is a fortune-teller. She tends to stay in the back alleys of the market area. Speak to her and show her the mark," Emrila instructed.

"How do you know I should do this?" Tagori asked.

"You are not the only one I can understand … nor are you the only one that has spoken with me," she said.

Tagori did as the dragon told him and entered the town, going to the alleys of the shopping district. Sure enough, a person was there sitting, focusing on some cards, her face covered in a veil. Tagori approached and spoke.

"Excuse me. Do you tell fortunes?"

"I do. My name is Serak," she said with a somewhat airy voice. "Come to have your fortune …?"

Her voice trailed off as she saw the marks Tagori showed her. "I see. So that's what you're after. Please have a seat."

Tagori sat opposite her. She grabbed a small box from under the table and pulled out a few bones. Holding the bones in her hand, she spoke to them and then handed them to Tagori.

"Cast them now."

Tagori raised his hands above the table and dropped the bones, which clacked into a random arrangement. Serak looked at the bones for a few moments before speaking.

"You have the signs of the usual tamer: long life, intricate mind, and your soul being intertwined with another. You will cause pain to everyone you know, you will make a discovery, and ... it looks as if you are the start of something ... I cannot tell what, though."

Tagori was meant to cause pain to all he knew? What did that mean? What did any of that mean?

"Now, the true reason you are here," Serak said. She reached back into the box and produced a scroll. "Follow this. You will require the item it will lead you to. Maybe this is the discovery you are meant to make."

Confused, Tagori unfurled the scroll to see a rather crude map. He knew the area the map depicted; it was Norico Island. The way the Grand River curved around both sides and the shape of the land gave it away. On the eastern edge of the island, a rocky outcropping was circled, the instructions "push" written next to it.

The map confused Tagori, but he decided that he would do as asked. "Thank you."

"Of course, tamer," she said, bowing. "Now, I must take my leave. I will await our next meeting."

Sarak gathered the bones and placed them into the box again. She then placed that box in a larger chest. This chest was small enough that it could be carried on her back by straps that wrapped around it. She walked off down the back streets, headed out of town.

Tagori went to the location on the map, the northeastern corner of the island, where Emrila joined him. He hoped that nobody would be on this side of the island to see them. They searched for only a half hour before coming to a location that might be what they were looking for. Tagori examined the outcropping. After pushing away some ivy, the underlying rock was smooth, almost unnaturally so.

He put his shoulder up to the rock and pushed on it. This smooth stone easily slid inward and down, revealing a tunnel with a staircase leading down. Tagori and Emrila glanced at each other, unsure of what dangers lurked inside. Tagori cautiously stepped inside, followed closely by Emrila. As soon as they reached the bottom of the stairs, the torches lit as they entered the chamber. The chamber had tall walls with a large arched ceiling. Six similar smaller chambers were attached to the far end of this chamber. The most curious part was the pedestal in the middle of the chamber. On it sat a sword. This sword was simple, nothing truly noticeable about it at first glance, though further inspection revealed a green tinted blade and a small green gem at the base of the hilt. The pedestal had an inscription that read "Wind's Blade," and upon reading the inscription aloud, clear yellow chains appeared around the blade where it touched the stand and burst, shattering like glass.

Tagori reached out and touched the hilt. Seeing it was safe, he wrapped his fingers around it. The marks on his arms appeared, glowing a warm white. He lifted the blade, feeling the weight of a true sword for the first time.

"*What are we supposed to do with that?*" Emrila asked.

"*I don't know. Does that fortune-teller intend for us to get involved in the war?*" Tagori replied.

Emrila and Tagori took the blade and left the strange shrine. When they emerged, a few dozen strange creatures were there to greet them. They were somewhat wolflike, though their limbs were thicker, more like those of a human's. They could stand on two or four legs just as easily. These creatures didn't seem like ones for conversation. Tagori readied his sword.

One of these creatures jumped at him, and he pointed his sword at it. Tagori felt a resistance in the blade as it was pushed into the creature's shoulder. Tagori pulled it out and tried to defend against another as it came at him, but it avoided and slashed Tagori's shoulder with its claw. The cut wasn't deep, though it did hurt. Tagori was surrounded, these creatures circling both him and Emrila, who seemed to be fending them off just fine with her tail and maw.

As two came at him at once, Tagori attacked the one in front of him just as someone cut down the one behind him. The man was dressed in nearly all black, with a cloth covering the majority of his face.

"You need to run," the man told Tagori.

"There is no way you can fight all of them alone," Tagori said.

"I can—now go!"

Reluctantly, Tagori did as he was told, Emrila following close behind him. Tagori hid behind a pile of large rocks, and as soon as he and Emrila were down, the man yelled, "Zenta Sosari Rioki," which was followed by a roar from some unknown source. After only a few moments, all noise ceased. A chilling silence followed.

Tagori looked at where the man had been fighting. He stood alone in a charred crater. The man turned to look at Tagori and fell as soon as they made eye contact. Tagori ran to the man, checking him for injuries. He seemed fine, though severely weakened.

"Tamer, I need you ... to do something," he said weakly. "Clear ... your mind ... and say ... 'Teriton' ... That spell ... will ... heal me ..."

Tagori did as instructed. A faint glow came from the marks on his arms as well as his hands as they hovered over the man. The longer he held this glow, the more painful his growing headache became.

"Stop," the man said.

Tagori removed his hands, and the glow faded.

"What ... what just happened?" Tagori said, stunned.

"You used magic," the man explained.

"Tell me, who are you?" Tagori asked.

"My name is ... Tarin."

"How did you kill those things?"

"I killed all the Kenthrish with the spell Living Flame Serpent. Don't get any ideas about trying to use it either," Tarin said.

"Oh? Why is that?"

"That spell is one of the more powerful ones. If you did use it, you would probably die from the strain."

"How could I use it?"

"Magic power is linked to your emotional state. The stronger you feel about a situation, the more powerful of a spell you can cast. Who knows—maybe you could have cast the spell."

"How do I keep that strength?"

"You just have to be unwavering," Tarin said. "I need to go. I've wasted too much time."

Tarin stood and walked to the southwest, toward the forest and across the bridge.

II

Tagori returned home as Emrila flew to the forest. He made sure to keep the new sword hidden, not wanting anyone to find out about it. Once he returned, he packed a bag for the trip he had planned to take with Roz. He lay on his bed, eager for the trip, though his mind was mostly on what Tarin had said about being unwavering. What would determine if he wavered?

He drifted off to sleep as he thought of what he could do to become stronger.

Tagori was lying down, and something seemed to be squeezing the breath out of him. He looked along his body, which was covered in black armor. A giant yellow claw was standing on top of him. It was connected to a large dragon that was looking down at him, flames rolling out of its mouth. Tagori brought his arms up to defend himself from the flame that he was sure were coming. He felt the weight of the dragon come off him. He opened his eyes to see why, only to find that Emrila had rammed the dragon.

Tagori stood up and looked around for anything he could use as a weapon. Only a few yards away, he saw a strange-looking blade. He picked it up. The sword was light in his hands. He thought he knew the sword—it felt somewhat familiar—but he was taken from his thoughts and drawn to the roar of the two dragons fighting. Tagori raised the sword above his head and ran to the yellow dragon. He saw the dragon tear a gash in Emrila's side and part of her leathery wing.

"No!" he exclaimed as he woke from the dream. "*Emrila!*"

He waited for a response.

"*Emrila!*" he screamed in his head.

He grabbed his sword and headed outside, yelling for the dragon to come to him.

"*Is everything all right?*" the dragon said as she emerged from the trees, shrouded in the night, her form nothing more than a starless blotch in the sky.

"*I wanted to ask you the same thing.*" Tagori told her. "*I'm sorry. I just had a nightmare.*"

"*Everything is all right,*" the dragon assured him.

Roz and Treth emerged from the house, having awakened after hearing the commotion that Tagori had caused.

Treth said, "Tagori, what's going ...? What is—"

Treth was cut off as a ball of fire fell from the sky, piercing the roof of the house, setting it ablaze. A second landed just north of the house, and a third landed right where Tagori's father and brother were standing.

A hot wind rushed past Tagori. They were fine. They had to be. Maybe this was still part of Tagori's nightmare. Tagori knew he was awake, though. This was a different kind of nightmare, one he would never wake up from.

He dropped to his knees. His family had just been killed. All he had was taken from him. He was now alone.

Three black creatures approached from the left of Tagori. Tagori could not see under the creatures' hooded cloaks, but he could see their black wings, muscular arms, and three-fingered hands. Each of them carried a long sword and a battle-ax.

Tarin stepped next to Tagori.

"They're gone. There's no way that they could have ..." Tagori choked up as he said the words.

"I'm going to need help fighting these Xen-Reths. Will you help?" Tarin asked.

Tagori stood, wiped away his tears, and readied his sword. "Let's do it."

"First I'm going to need you to hold your hand over your sword like this," Tarin said, holding his middle two fingers together and his other fingers apart. "And say 'Erono Riorin Ignight.'"

Tagori did as he was told, repeating the words and feeling the strain of magic. The blade of Tagori's sword wrapped itself in a bright warm red flame. The fire was greater than Tarin remembered seeing in quite some time. Despite its intensity, the heat did not burn Tagori, though it did warm him ever so slightly.

"Tagori ... what sort of resolve ...?" Tarin began, stopping after seeing him look at the creatures with determination in his eyes. Tarin held his hand over his own sword, saying, "Erono Yarega, freeze." His sword burst with a water jet and then froze into a pillar of ice. "Don't let your guard down; these things will try anything to get you. Good luck."

As Tarin finished, Tagori ran at one of the Xen-Reths, slashing just as he reached it. It moved just enough to dodge the blade. The fire attached to the blade came around and passed through the Xen-Reth, burning where it touched, though Tagori knew it would only be on the surface. If Tagori wanted to do any damage, he would need to connect with his blade.

The Xen-Reth flew into the air, readying its ax. It pointed its sword at him as it dove though the air. Tagori brought his sword up to defend himself against the attack and closed his eyes. He felt nothing for a few seconds, and he opened his eyes out of curiosity. The Xen-Reth was trapped in Emrila's powerful jaw, its body now limp and lifeless.

"*We fight together!*" Emrila said.

Tagori agreed as they looked at each other. They knew they would be all right as long as they stuck together.

Tarin fought another of these creatures, like the one already dead at their feet. Tagori ran to assist him but was not able to reach him. The Xen-Reth readied both its weapons in a combined attack. Would Tarin be able to defend against the attacks? Tagori didn't want to wait to find out. He held his hand out and yelled the spell Rioria. A ball of fire flew from his hand and collided with the Xen-Reth, causing it to fall over. Tarin quickly stabbed the Xen-Reth, finishing it off.

"Tagori," Tarin said, approaching and sheathing his sword, "how did you know that word?"

"It just came to me," Tagori said. He lifted his sword and asked, "How do I put this out?"

"Sever the magic to it."

Tagori focused for a second, trying to feel exactly where the magic was coming from. He felt it and quickly severed the flow.

"If you want the flame back, all you have to do is say ignite. Meet me back here tomorrow; bring your sword."

"What do I do in the meantime?" Tagori said, looking at the remains of his home. The fires had almost burned themselves out. "My home was destroyed."

"Your house was destroyed. Your home is fine." Tarin threw Tagori a small pouch that clinked as he caught it. "There are one hundred ryngs in there. Use it to get a room at the inn and something to eat in the morning."

"Tarin, I don't know why, but you seem familiar in some way," Tagori said, "like a long-lost friend."

Tarin looked shocked. "I've never met you before yesterday. I don't know why you would think that."

"Well, wherever you go," Tagori told Tarin, "good luck."

Tagori got a room at the inn, surprised that he could still get one this late at night. As he was lying in bed, he thought about why Tarin seemed familiar. He couldn't imagine the reason. His mind wandered back to his lost family. Why had they been the ones attacked? It may have been more appropriate to wonder why Tagori himself had not been the one killed. What was he going to do now? Without his family, he had nothing. He was alone. Eventually, Tagori's tears led him to sleep.

He awoke about midday, hoping that everything that had happened the previous night was a dream, but unfortunately, he was in the room he had rented.

"Emrila, I'm going to whatever is left of my house."

"Be careful," she warned. "Something might still be out for you."

"I know. I'll have the sword with me. You'll also be close enough to help me, won't you?"

"You can't always rely on me."

"Are you admitting to being unreliable?"

"I'll let you think what you want of that."

With that, Tagori left the inn. When he arrived at what was left of his home, he was saddened. He walked on the ashes as he looked for anything that could be of use. Most everything had been burned and was unusable or simply not worth keeping.

Tagori would practically need to start his life over. Maybe he should go to Areno and find a job. But he was sixteen and still didn't have a trade. He couldn't stay in Norico. Every day would just remind him of what had been taken away from him.

The Xen-Reths must have been targeting someone in his family, but who ... and why? What did he have that they wanted? What if they'd attacked him because he was a new tamer? No one should know that he was—unless it was the individual who left the egg for him. He had so many questions that needed to be answered.

"What are you doing?" Tarin asked, approaching from the south.

"Seeing if I can salvage anything," Tagori said.

"Everything has been pretty well burnt. Although …" Tarin moved into the ashes. He pulled out a metal ring that had once been used as a door handle. "You could use this."

"Oh? What for?"

"You need a sheath for your sword," Tarin explained. "Just tie this to your belt."

Tagori looked at the ring. He could keep this little piece of what his life had been. He found a small piece of rope and tied the ring to his belt. He slipped his sword through the ring with quite a bit of room to spare.

"How is your swordsmanship?" Tarin asked.

"Why?" Tagori asked.

"You are going to need to defend yourself," Tarin said.

"Why do you say that?" Tagori asked.

"You know the king is trying to limit the power of the people. He does this in any way that he can. If a tamer joined him, the people would be more inclined to follow him, and even if you refuse to join him, killing a tamer would make the people fear him. In fact, the Xen-Reths came from the castle," Tarin explained. "You weren't planning on joining him now, were you?"

"No. The empire has already hurt me."

"They have hurt us all," Tarin said. "Do you want to be trained to use that sword?"

After a moment of thinking it over, Tagori responded, "Yes, I need to."

"You don't need to do anything."

"No, this is something I need to do."

"Gather anything you might need and meet me at the north bridge in an hour."

Tagori retrieved his bag from the inn and went to the market. He bought a change of clothes and some fruit, also taking some dried meat from his father's shop. The well-memorized butcher shop reminded him of the previous night. Simply stepping inside made him feel as though his heart were being crushed. He then walked down the main street one more time before heading to the north bridge. Tarin already stood next to the bridge, looking at the town in the distance.

After a long pause, Tarin said, "I've tried to never get too attached to a place. I always end up leaving it. But this place is different. It feels like … home. I always feel like this when I leave this place. Norico, I will return eventually."

Tagori felt the same way about leaving. After another few minutes, Tarin turned away and had Tagori follow him across the bridge. When the city was well out of sight, Emrila joined them.

"So where are we going?" Tagori asked.

"The Gilrund."

Tagori knew the Gilrund as the group that was attempting to dethrone the king, though the way they went about doing so made many question their purpose. Maybe the creatures that attacked him had been sent from the Gilrund. That seemed impossible though, as Tarin had fought against them.

"What?" Tagori said, shocked. "You've been with them?"

"Of course. I was to look after you," Tarin said.

"What? How did you know it would be me?"

"The Gilrund's eyes are everywhere. All we had to do was to look for strange behaviors. Don't think yourself special, though. It wasn't you specifically I was to look out for—but anyone that may be a tamer or need protection from the empire."

"What can you tell me about the Gilrund?"

"We'll take anyone who wants justice in the land. We have smiths and farmers, tailors and bakers, mages and swordsmen, and they have skills greater than you could imagine. We have never had a tamer though. It's not like there have been any recently."

"What's our first destination?"

"Kyata. We need to bring someone with us. He has been away for a while and needs to check in. There is a town between here and Kyata, Verton. It's not big, but we can pick up supplies and save the ones we have. We'll be able to reach it before the sun sets."

For the longest time, they traveled in silence. Emrila made sure to question whether Tarin could be trusted. He assured her that he had saved Tagori at the risk of his own life, so he couldn't be all bad. However, the fact that Tarin kept most of his face hidden concerned Tagori. What could he be hiding?

"How does that weapon magic work?" Tagori asked.

"There are many elements that can be put on a weapon. Each one of those has a different ability. Your flame, for example, is like a whip. The ice on mine creates crystals in the air that dissipate after a few moments. It's dangerous because it can even create them inside of something." Tarin looked off into the distance. "You can see Verton just over the hill here."

Tagori had never been anywhere but Norico, so this was a chance to see what it was truly like in another city. They made their way to the market and bought some supplies, and then they went to the inn to turn in for the night. Tagori paid with the remainder of what Tarin had given them.

Tagori woke in the morning to find that Tarin had left. Tagori walked out into the streets to see if he could get a chance to look around this small town. It seemed just like Norico, though much busier. He stared down the streets before feeling a hand on his shoulder. Tagori spun around with a hand on his blade, only to see Tarin behind him.

"Where did you run off to?" Tagori asked.

"There were some things I needed to see to, nothing you should worry about," he responded. "Ready to leave?"

"I am. Do we have enough supplies?"

"We have plenty."

"Then by all means, let's go."

Together they left the city, turning to make their trip across the country of Sonnon. As soon as the city was out of sight, Emrila joined them. They needed to rest every couple of hours because of Tagori, but Tarin was always ready to go. He kept moving in one way or another, walking, swinging his sword, or doing some other activity. Emrila kept asking questions, which Tagori had to relay.

Near the end of the day, they approached the city. The gates were closed, and nobody stood near them. Tarin pounded his fist on the wooden door in frustration.

"We'll have to sleep in the protection of the forest," Tarin said.

"Oh?"

"The gates are closed; they won't be opening until the morning."

They walked off to the nearby forest in the northwest. Before falling asleep, they ate a small meal. Exhausted, Tagori fell asleep easily.

"Tagori, wake up. Kenthrish are attacking," Emrila warned.

Tagori rolled, grabbing his sword as he did so. He rose and stabbed at the Kenthrish, but it had moved.

"Ignite," Tagori said, trying to call on the flame he had put into the blade. Nothing happened. As he parried an attack, he said the word again and had the same result. "Tarin, didn't you say that word would bring back the flame?"

"It should have," Tarin said, fighting off a Kenthrish of his own. "Worry about fighting right now!"

Tagori turned his attention away from his blade and focused on his enemy. He slashed at the enemy, but it dodged and retaliated every time. Tagori, dodging a few of the Kenthrish's attacks, was becoming more exhausted with each attack. As it jumped to deliver the final blow, Tagori felt something fly past his shoulder. Then he heard the creature scream in pain. Its body lay motionless on the ground, an arrow sticking out of its head and heart. Tagori turned around to see a person with a bow on the wall of the city. Tarin had turned around too.

The man jumped off the wall, a height of about ten feet, and began running toward them. He had a packed quiver on his back as well as a bow in hand. His straight hair, a brown so deep that it was almost black, bounced into his eyes as he ran.

"Arrow," Tarin yelled, "nice shot!"

"Thanks," he said as he met with Tarin. "But I was a little off. I'm pretty sure I grazed bone. Who's this with you?"

"My name is Tagori," he said.

"Could he be …?" Arrow asked.

"The new tamer," Tarin finished. The inflection of his voice seemed to say something more.

"I see. Well, my name is Darith. Everyone calls me Arrow, though."

"How did you know to come here?" Tagori asked.

"I was just walking along the wall when I saw you," Arrow said.

"In the morning, we will go through town to get your things and then make our way to Kyata," Tarin explained.

"There are some brothers that would like to join us living in Kyata. Some friends of mine," Arrow said.

"We will pick them up when we go through the city.

Arrow replied, "In the morning then."

III

Tagori woke up sore from the night's battle. Arrow and Tarin were already awake, waiting for Tagori. They were talking and eating a simple breakfast.

"Tagori," Arrow said, "let me see your sword.

He handed the blade to Arrow, who began looking it over, getting to know every delicate curve of the blade. The gem was the cause of much scrutiny as Arrow tried to determine why such a gem would be placed in a sword. The fact that it had been inset in the blade caused him to believe that there was some significance in it.

"Where was this blade found?"

"Just outside Norico. There was a strange underground shrine," Tagori explained.

"Tarin, I think this is Zak'reen," Arrow said.

"It's part of the Zak'reen series?"

Tagori had heard the name but couldn't remember where. He remembered then that the founder of Norico had used a blade of the same name.

"Tarin, that was the blade used by Kaireg, wasn't it?" Tagori asked.

"I ... I don't think so," Tagori said.

"Well, the tamer Kaireg, along with his companions, defeated the evil wizard Metenro," Tarin told Tagori. "After that, the group separated and Kaireg found himself in what is now Norico. The land was barren. There was no life to be seen for leagues. Kaireg sacrificed himself to bring life to the land. He was turned into the tree in the center of the town. Some of his friends came looking for him, but all they found was his sword in the grasp of a wooden hand. They knew that he sacrificed himself, so they took his sword and put it in a shrine in the newly formed forest. I don't know what happened to the rest of his arsenal, though."

"So that is how Norico came to be," Tagori said.

"Tarin, what do you think the crystal is for?" Arrow asked.

"No clue."

Arrow handed the blade back to Tagori.

"Arrow, can you tell me anything about the dragons and humans?'

"I don't know much, but I do know that there used to be thousands of dragons; however, humans eventually stopped needing them. Humans just learned to evolve," Arrow told him.

"We evolved past their need? I don't think I will ever evolve past needing ...," Tagori began, but he stopped speaking when he saw the blade of his sword retract into the hilt. The small green gem fell out of the hilt. They sat there and stared at it before Tagori picked the crystal up.

"Tagori, put the crystal back in place and say 'Evolve Ax,'" Arrow said.

Taking the hilt from Arrow, Tagori did as instructed. Immediately, a shaft came out of the hilt, growing to about three feet. A simple single triangular blade came out of the tip. The hilt itself had changed; the cross guard rotated up, creating a fine straight shaft. The result was a simple hatchet.

"Looks like Kaireg didn't have an arsenal but a single weapon that could become anything," Arrow said, clearly excited from the discovery.

"We need to keep moving," Tarin urged.

"We just found Kaireg's weapons, and you don't care at all," Arrow pointed out.

"No, I do. Once we get Tagori safe, we will have plenty of time to dwell on these things."

"True. It's not as if we can't examine it as we move. Let's be on our way."

The three of them headed into town to pick up Arrow's things before immediately setting off toward the Grand River. Emrila joined them as soon as the city was out of view. Arrow was thrilled to see her and examine a living dragon for himself.

"Arrow, is there anything that you could teach me about magic?"

"What do you know already?"

"Only that it comes from the strength of the mind."

"That's true, but the strength of the spell is affected by your frame of mind. For example, if you have a stronger will, you will cast a stronger spell compared to someone with a weak will. Now, because the language is so vast, most people choose to use only one or two elements, becoming proficient with using only those and knowing what each command does. tamers would probably have enough time to learn a few more elements. Because they used one element, they became known as elementalists. For example, I can use fire; Tarin can use light. Every time he uses a spell, he takes a big chance. If he said a spell wrong, he could die. With your tamer marks, you can cast more powerful spells, even more so if you two are linked."

"What do you mean linked?" Tagori asked.

"I'm not quite sure, but tamers are known to be able to use their dragons' strength to help their spells."

"Should I become an elementalist?" he asked Emrila.

"It would only be natural, wouldn't it?" she responded.

"Which one should I choose?"

"I do enjoy the air."

"That's only because you can fly."

"Maybe that is the reason," she said with a laugh.

"Arrow, is it possible to use the air?"

"I suppose. Most of the wind spells I know aren't that strong, though. From what I understand, it's also one of the vastest series in the language," Arrow explained. "Tarin, do you have any air spells for Tagori?"

"Air? Interesting. I do know one. Tagori, try the spell Ginariun," Tarin said.

"Tarin, isn't that …?"

"Let's just see how he does, Arrow," Tarin said.

Tagori focused his mind, touching the flow of magic that had slowly begun to become more familiar to him. When he spoke the word, the wind spun around him, gathering into his hand, compressing. The air became visible, radiating a light green. As Tagori moved his right hand, the orb moved with it, maintaining a constant distance above his hand.

Tarin and Arrow stared at it in disbelief, too stunned to say anything.

"What's wrong?"

"That wasn't supposed to happen. The wind was just meant to swirl around you," Arrow explained.

"It was?"

Emrila's grumbling pulled Tagori's attention from anything Tarin or Arrow may have said.

"We're being watched," she said.

"From where?"

"The trees."

Sure enough, looking amongst the trees revealed eyes of a few kenthrish. Tagori pulled his sword out with left hand. As one kenthrish jumped, Tagori tried to cut it, but it dodged by turning to the side. It quickly recovered and scratched at Tagori, catching his arm. Tagori brought his arm up to swat away the creature, and the ball of air came around, hitting the creature and knocking it away.

"That spell is a gift; use it well," Tarin said.

"Tarin, move," Arrow told Tarin. Arrow strung his bow. "Riorogin Nentreth." The tip of the arrow started on fire. Arrow shot it at a group of kenthrish, hitting one of them in the shoulder. The kenthrish screamed in pain. "Kon Kon," Arrow said. The arrow exploded, killing several of the beasts. Tagori lunged at one of them, swinging the orb. It hit the beast, throwing it back. Tagori turned around to see a kenthrish lunge at him. Emrila caught it in her jaws, killing it.

"*I'll protect you,*" she told him.

With their numbers dwindling, they retreated into the forest from which they had emerged. Tagori breathed a sigh of relief.

"Finally!" he said. "Arrow, what did you do to them?"

"What do you mean?"

"That spell you cast … What was it?"

"Oh! That was my special spell: Firebomb Projectile. After I fire it, I say 'Boom boom.' The damage is … well, you saw what it's like."

"Now, about this …?" Tagori said, looking at the orb.

"Sever the magic to it," Arrow told him.

"Just like with the sword spell," Tarin said.

Tagori held his hand out and focused on the flow of magic. Then he severed it. The wind flowed around Tagori once more before dispersing. He felt refreshed by the wind.

They moved forward, wanting to reach the next city as quickly as possible. After about an hour, they could see the city walls.

"Tarin, take a look at this!" Arrow said.

The three of them looked to the city, only to see a small group of soldiers outside of it.

"What are we going to do?" Tagori asked.

"We do nothing."

"What about Arrow's friends?"

"They should be fine as long as they keep their mouths shut about the Gilrund," Tarin said.

"More reason for us to get in there," Arrow said. "They aren't the best at keeping secrets."

"Great," Tarin said. "We could slip around to the north and try to enter from there. Find them and leave."

"Fine, you two go. I'll catch up," Arrow said.

Tarin and Tagori walked to the north gate, where they entered the city. Arrow could be seen behind them.

"Tagori, he cast a spell. Be wary of Arrow."

"What did it do?"

"I don't know. It seemed to be targeted at himself. Just be careful around him."

"I will. You don't need to worry about that."

Once they had all entered the city, Arrow joined them, explaining his friends' appearance.

"Tarin, you take the south side of the town," Arrow said. "Tagori, you take the west; I'll take the north. Let's meet back here in two hours. We are looking for Dago, who usually has a big sword or two knives on his left side, and Enro, who should have a small sword or a pickax."

Tagori's result proved fruitless. He saw someone in the square with a long sword on his back and approached the man.

"Excuse me, is your name Dago?"

"No, it's not."

"Sorry to bother you, then," Tagori said.

He turned, looking to the sun and seeing that the two hours had almost passed.

"You are looking for a man named Dago?" the man he had mistaken for Dago asked.

"Yes. Do you know him?"

"By order of the king, you are under arrest for suspicion of treason."

Tagori pulled his sword out.

"Don't make this harder than it needs to be, kid," the man said.

Tagori put his hand over his sword as Tarin had taught him and said, "Erono Ginari, vortex." The wind once again swirled around him. Then a funnel of swirling air formed around his sword and the marks on his arms began to glow.

"A spell caster?" the man said. Upon noticing Tagori's marks, he revised his evaluation. "A tamer!"

Tagori slashed at the guard, who was blown back by the intense wind that came from Tagori's sword.

The guard landed on his feet and then came rushing Tagori. When Tagori slashed up with his sword, a wave of air shot out of it, hitting the guard and pushing him into a stall. Tagori's arms stopped glowing when he sheathed his sword. He looked around at the crowd to see them all staring at him.

Tagori ran back to the rendezvous point, where Arrow was waiting with Dago, a stout, strong man with long blond hair. He was wearing a cloak that covered his entire body.

"We need to get out of the city," Tagori said, out of breath.

"What happened?"

"I was arrested and fought back. They know about me now!"

"They what!"

"I know," Tagori said. "What else was I supposed to do?"

"You're right. Where are Enro and Tarin?"

"Enro will be here," Dago said. "I just know he will."

Tarin came running around a corner, a glowing orb in each hand. He turned and threw the orbs out of sight. He went down on one knee, breathing heavily. The three ran over to aid him. A soldier walked toward them, a large battle-ax in hand.

"Are all of you roaches allied with the rebels?" the man said, laughing. "Now I can kill all of you at once."

"You'll never kill us," Dago said as he threw his cloak off and drew his knives. "Volt."

His knives became electrical, crackling with energy. He jumped for the guard, who blocked Dago's first strike with his axes. Dago turned around, still holding the ax with one of his knives and stabbing at the guard's side with his other.

With the guard's attention still on Dago, Tagori drew his sword and ran at the man. He swung his ax at Tagori, who raised his sword to block the attack, and as the two weapons collided, Tagori's sword changed to a shield. Dago took this opportunity to attack, slipping behind the man's ax and cutting into his side. The soldier was hurt but still willing to fight.

The guard began to rush Arrow, but a man took him down. The man stood with his pickax out, holding it where he had hit the guard.

"It's over now," the man said. He walked up to the guard, who was getting up. "Secthoren Lachret," he said, and the guard's legs froze in a block of ice. "Secthoren Lachrep," he then said, and the guard's arms froze. "Secthoren Segartor—good-bye." The guard froze solid. The man came around with his pickax and shattered the guard with one swift blow.

Dago ran over to Tarin and began to heal him. The man began to walk toward Tagori, who stood guard, pointing his sword at the man.

"It's okay. I'm Enro; I'm with Dago," the man said.

Enro was just as tall as Dago, if not slightly taller. His hair had been cut short, keeping it well out of his eyes. His build was similar to Enro's, though with a little more bulk around his bones, making him appear sturdier than Dago.

Tagori lowered his sword and sheathed it in the ring. He looked this new man over and saw the similarities to Dago, though shorter and younger looking. He had long blond hair as opposed to Dago's brown, which hung in front of his eyes.

"We have to get out of here now!" Arrow said.

"It is getting rather treacherous," Tarin said.

"General Nebin!" a strange voice said.

The group turned to see a small group of soldiers standing at the end of the street.

"Who did this?" a soldier with a long red cape asked. "You … You're the rebels! Men, arrest them!"

They all turned to run, hoping to lose the guards in the city, but the streets seemed to be devoid of any activity.

"Tagori, can you use a spell?" Dago asked.

"If it's weak, then yes, I should be able to."

"Everyone, the spell is 'Bentero'!" Dago said.

As Tagori spoke the word, everything rushed past him, faster than he thought possible. They soon saw the city's gate and ran through it. They continued running until the city was out of sight. They rested on the hill, and Emrila immediately joined them.

"How did you find us?" Tagori asked Enro.

"I noticed a scuffle, so I thought that I would help out. It was only after I recognized Dago that I understood who you were," he explained.

"We should continue moving," Tarin said, standing and still breathing heavily.

"Where are we headed?" Dago asked.

"To the Gilrund. That's the reason we were in the city," Arrow explained. "You said you wanted to join it, didn't you?"

"Well, I guess … It's not as if I'm able to go home now anyway," Dago said.

"What do you mean?" Enro asked

"The soldiers were in the city for us. They probably have our house watched," Dago explained.

"You probably have a point," Enro said.

"*I don't like Enro,*" Emrila told Tagori.

"*Why not?*"

"*There is something about him. It might be his smell.*"

"*He's fine. You just have to get to know him.*"

"*All right, but don't say that I didn't warn you,*" she grumbled.

The small group of people and the large dragon headed off to the east, following the river.

"Tarin, how did you find out about the Gilrund?" Tagori asked.

"I'm one of the founders—Arrow, three other people, and myself," he replied.

"So who is in charge of it now?"

"That's a complicated matter; we have the other three founders on a board, making the important decisions, and if they can't agree on a course of action, then there are the seven elders that we have in the northeast mountains," Tarin explained. "They have been elected to decide what course the resistance will take as a whole. It's all rather complicated politics."

Tagori let this sink in as they walked. Once he was sure he understood the basic process they went through, his mind began to go over what had already happened this day.

"Enro, what was that spell you used against the soldier?" Tagori asked.

"That was a spell I was taught to use only in an emergency. It's called Ice Grave, and it nearly always kills who it is cast on. It's composed of three spells: freeze legs, freeze arms, and freeze solid."

They continued to talk about how the spell worked in detail, but not much else was said between anyone else. Tagori still couldn't believe that he had left Norico. His small town was all he had known, but now he was participating in the war. Battles were sure to flare up now, especially after people began to learn that a tamer had emerged. Tagori thought about what he was causing.

"Do not worry—this isn't because of you. This would have happened regardless. Just because one person appears does not mean that the two factions will begin fighting differently," Emrila said.

She was right, but Tagori couldn't stop blaming himself. Ultimately, both sides would fight for his allegiance. Was he even sure that he wanted to choose a side? What else could he do? He couldn't leave the country to fight itself now that there was something that he could do to affect the outcome.

The Grand River appeared on their right, a sign that it would not take much longer to reach the Gilrund, or so Tagori had been told.

"When should we see the Gilrund?" Tagori asked.

"It'll be another few days, even if we travel through the night," Arrow said.

"Any towns between us?"

"Just one: Port Hikran. We won't get there till tomorrow."

The group continued until the sun fell below the horizon. Just as Tagori was feeling thoroughly exhausted, they found a sheltered place in the woods nearby, set up a camp, and went to sleep.

They continued their journey the next morning, Tagori's legs sore from all the exercise over the past few days. They soon found Port Hikran. The large city walls told that it was well protected. There were several large ships at the docks, all carrying different cargo. They entered the city, looking at the amazing architecture. A large tower stood in the center of the town.

"We'll meet at the inn and stay for the night," Tarin said.

"What will we do in the meantime?" Tagori asked.

"Stay out of trouble," Arrow said. "Other than that, you're free to do as you please."

Tagori took some time to search through some of the shops to look for anything that may be useful on the rest of the trip. Finding nothing, he headed to the tavern to eat. Once he emerged, he noticed that the sun had nearly set, and he made his way to the inn. Tarin and Dago were already waiting outside, and Arrow could be seen running from down the street.

"Where's Enro?" Tagori asked.

"He'll show up later," Dago said. "Let's get our rooms."

Tagori awoke with a start, a result of a bad dream. Seeing that Arrow had already left the room, he went to check on everyone else. Dago and Tarin had already awakened, but Enro's bed seemed to have been untouched. Tagori walked to the lobby to find Arrow, Tarin, and Dago.

"Where's Enro?" Tagori asked.

"He never came back," Dago said.

"I'll ask if he has been seen," Tarin said. He walked to the desk and spoke with the woman behind it. She said a few words to Tarin and then searched under the desk for something, producing a note and handing it to Tarin, who read it as he walked back.

"Enro has been captured," Tarin said definitively. "Taken to a tower in the north."

"That can't be," Dago said, grabbing the note from Tarin to read it.

"We have to get him out," Arrow said.

"Our objective now is to get Tagori to the ... the alliance," Tarin said, not wanting to mention the Gilrund in such close quarters.

"What? Are you just going to abandon him?" Tagori asked.

"No, we will leave immediately after we deliver you," Tarin said.

"Who's to say what will happen to him in that time?" Tagori replied. "How much farther do we even have to go? A few days? He could be dead by the time you find him."

"Tagori, drop it," Dago said. The pain he experienced from that simple phrase was evident in his face. Dago had just put Tagori above his own brother "We'll get you to where you're going and then save him."

"Fine," Tagori said defeated. "Then let's get going."

They gathered their few remaining things and left the city, heading north along the river. The land gradually became rockier and rougher, and soon there was a sheer fall down to the river on one side of them and badlands on the other. Tagori scanned the landscape, looking for any sort of civilization, but there was nothing but a single white pillar off in the distance.

"Tarin, are there any castles around here?" Tagori asked.

"None that I know of. Why?"

"What does that look like?" Tagori said, pointing to the tower.

Tarin followed Tagori's finger to the tower, staring at it with wide eyes. "We will explore it later."

"That note did say that Enro was taken to the north, didn't it?"

"What did we already explain to you?"

"Are you ready to fly?"

"What are you up to?" the dragon asked.

"We have to look. Standing around won't save him."

"Why are you so intent on saving him?"

"He protected us, and he is Dago's brother. We have to."

"All right, whenever you're ready."

"I'm going to see if he's in there myself," Tagori said.

Tagori wrapped his hands around Emrila's neck as she leaped into the air. He almost fell off as she flapped her wings to gain altitude. Once she was high enough, she glided toward the tower, flipping to help Tagori get in a better position on her back.

"Tarin, we have to go after them," Arrow said, "They don't know what's in that tower."

"Are you saying that you do?" Tarin asked.

"I have a better idea than they do."

Tagori was enjoying the feeling of the wind in his face. He spread his arms to get the full feeling of the wind. Everything felt amazing, from the cool air to the feel of the strain on the dragon's wings.

"Enjoying yourself?"

"I am."

"Remember why we're doing this."

"Right. We need to get Enro back."

"How are we going to get inside?" she asked as she circled the top of the tower.

"What do you mean?"

"The entrance will be guarded. You won't be able to just walk inside."

"Right … What do you suggest?"

"I suggest we land so I can rest my wings. I'm not used to your weight."

"What are you trying to say?" Tagori said jokingly.

She landed on the top of the tower to give them a moment to look around and think of a solution to their problem. Perhaps Tagori could slip in a window. No, that wouldn't work, because he would still have no way to escape. An escape would be the largest problem. There were plenty of ways to enter the tower but only one way to exit … unless they had help. Would coming in from the top be the easiest way?

"*Think we could come in from here?*" Tagori asked.

"*Where?*"

"*The roof here.*"

"*Do you have an idea how to pass through stone?*"

"*We make an opening.*"

Tagori pulled his sword out and held it in front of him. "Evolve, hammer!"

As he said this, his blade began to morph, changing into a large hammer. He swung it over his head and brought it down on the tower, breaking off a chunk of stone. He swung again, this time breaking a larger piece off. With each successive hit, Tagori came closer to breaking through the stone. Finally, a section fell away allowing him access to the chamber that lay below.

"*You will have to carry us out of here. Are you all right with that?*"

"*I am … as long as you live.*"

"*Then I'm going. I'll be in contact.*"

With that, Tagori looked into the hole, into the chamber that would lead him to Enro. Without another moment of hesitation, he jumped in.

IV

Tagori hit the floor, creating a thump that echoed through the room. The room was large and had a marble floor. There were swords on display on the wall and a desk near one wall. Opposite the desk was a staircase leading down into the guts of the tower. Tagori started running down the steps. On both sides of him were prison cells; very few people were in them, however. Tagori continued down the long flight of stairs until he reached a door.

Tagori pushed the door open slowly, seeing two burly men inside. The chamber seemed to be for information gathering. Information from this room would have been extracted by any means necessary.

The men noticed Tagori, grabbed hatchets off the wall, and came at him. Tagori quickly closed the door, hearing the hatchets bury themselves in the wooden door. He kicked it open, hoping to hit one of them with the door. Unfortunately, his tactic only made one of them stumble, and the second swung his hatchet at Tagori. He rolled under it, entering the room. The second managed to pull his hatchet out of the door, and they attacked Tagori in unison. He pulled his sword out to defend against the attacks, flinching at the prospect of being hit. He heard metal clashing against metal yet felt no resistance from his blade.

Tagori opened his eyes and saw Tarin standing before him, blocking one ax with his sword and holding the second ax steady with his other.

"Don't you ever do as you're told?" Tarin said as he pushed the axes away. "Now go look for Enro."

Tagori just stood there, blade ready at his side. "No. I'm not going to see another of my friends get hurt."

"Still ignoring orders," Tarin said, almost laughing. "Fine, we'll take them together."

"Can we join?" Arrow said, appearing in the doorway, flaming arrow strung. "Move." Arrow loosed the weapon. It sailed through the air, burying itself in the side of one of the men. The man tried frantically to pull the arrow out. His ally grabbed the arrow as well, trying to dislodge the bomb. As they were distracted, Arrow cast a second spell, setting the two men ablaze, slowly killing them.

"Let's go up. He wasn't in any of the cells below," Tarin said.

They all moved up the steps that Tagori had come from. Dago stopped about halfway up, looking into a cell. The others went to his side, examining the cell as well. Enro sat hunched over on one side.

"How do we get him out?"

"With the key, but where would it be?"

"Either in the entrance or where we just fought."

"I'll go check," Dago said, running down the stairs.

"We need ... to take ... him with ...," Enro began weakly.

In the opposite corner was a man sitting in the same state as Enro.

"Who are you?"

"Verag," he said, disoriented.

"They've been drugged," Arrow said, "most likely to suppress their spell casting."

Dago came running back up the stairs, a key ring in his hand. They fumbled with the keys as they attempted to find the correct one for the lock. Once they found it, they went inside the cell and helped Enro out of it.

"You have to take Verag," Enro said in his drugged state.

The others shot glances at each other before deciding to comply with Enro's request. Dago descended with Enro, and Arrow descended with Verag. Tagori ascended the stairs, wanting to fly with Emrila. Tagori reached the top of the stairs as he entered the office again. Something seemed strange though, out of place, but Tagori didn't know why.

"Do you know how long it's going to take to fix that hole?" a voice said. It was low and resonating. It had a tone of leadership and sent a chill up Tagori's spine.

Tagori looked all around the room. His eyes eventually fixed on the chair behind the desk. He prepared to draw his sword and circled around to the front of the chair, which was turned away from him. When he got around it, he held his blade up in preparation to stab whoever it was.

"You're looking in the wrong place for me," the man whispered in Tagori's ear.

When Tagori turned around, he was punched in the stomach. He was tossed across the floor. Tagori forced himself to stand up. He readied his sword to attack, facing the tall silver-haired man.

The man's muscles rippled underneath his shirt, though they weren't being accentuated purposefully. His strong jawbone accentuated his eerie smile.

"Because I feel it is polite to let victims know who killed them, allow me to introduce myself. I am Icharro," he said. The man started rushing at Tagori, who rotated on his foot and slashed as he came around, hitting Icharro in the back. This set Icharro off balance, but he vaulted off his hand and landed on his feet near a sword display. He pulled the sword off the wall.

"Emrila, get Tarin here. I need his help," Tagori told her.

"I'll see what I can do," Emrila said.

Tagori successfully blocked most of his strikes, but the ones he wasn't blocking were hitting him hard. He knew that he couldn't withstand much more of the assault. He was hit once more, and as his eyes opened, he saw a shield. He had an idea.

"Evolve, shield," Tagori said. The green blade contorted into the shape of a shield.

"What sort of sorcery is that?" Icharro asked.

This light shield allowed Tagori to block most of the attacks directed at him. As soon as Tagori saw an attack coming, he moved his arm and knocked away the blow. A loud thud distracted Icharro enough to allow Tagori to hit Icharro with his shield, dazing him.

Moments later, Tarin fell from the hole, calling out "Freeze!" as he fell. A jet of water flowed from the cross guard of his drawn sword, which then froze into the frozen blade that Tarin had used back in Norico. Tagori took the time to change his shield back to the sword he knew.

Icharro recovered, wiping the blood from his nose. He ran at Tagori, punching him and sending him flying into the wall. Then Icharro spun around in an attempt at hitting Tarin, but he blocked this attack with one move of his blade. He pushed Icharro's blade into the floor, stood on it, and pointed his sword at Icharro's.

"Yarera beku." A ball of ice burst from his sword, freezing Icharro's to the floor. He jumped away and pointed his hand at Icharro, saying "Solarden Kibiken Sizvenderu." A ball of light appeared in his palm, and he threw it at Icharro.

There was a tense moment as they waited for the smoke from the blast to clear. Tagori saw a black figure move in the smoke. It quickly began emerging from it.

"Tarin, guard yourself," Tagori shouted.

Tarin saw Icharro emerge from the smoke. Tarin began running as well, ready to strike with his sword. As they neared each other, their swords moved, Icharro's blade broken in half. Blood immediately fell on the stone floor.

Icharro stood up straight and tall, but Tarin's body fell in a heap, almost motionless. Tagori couldn't believe what he'd just seen; Tarin couldn't be beaten.

Tagori screamed as he ran, sword extended, at his foe. Icharro pushed away Tagori's sword and then kicked him across the room. Tagori slid on the polished floor until he hit the wall. He thought that he should run, but he knew that he had to take Tarin with him. Tagori stood up.

"Don't you know when to stay down, boy?" Icharro asked.

"Yes, I do know when to stay down," Tagori said.

"Then why don't you?" Icharro asked him.

"This isn't the time to give up. I know I can win." Tagori lifted his head; his determination was visible in his eyes. He held his arm out and said the name of the spell Ginariun.

"What do you intend to do with a useless spell like that?" Icharro said.

"Useless?" Tagori replied.

Icharro realized that the air was doing more than just swirling around the room. Tagori ran at him once more.

Icharro attacked with his broken sword. Tagori raised the hand that the orb was in, catching Icharro's attack and stopping it. With his other hand, he stabbed Icharro in the stomach. Icharro grabbed Tagori's hand that the sword was in, pulled out the sword, and threw him across the room. Tagori recovered in the air, using the orb to help him regain his balance. He skidded to a stop.

"You'll die yet," Icharro said. He threw his sword at Tagori, who instinctively put his hand up in defense. The orb caught the blade. Tagori pushed the orb in the direction of Icharro. The broken sword flew straight at Icharro and hit him in the heart, but Icharro was still alive. He pulled the sword out of himself and started to limp over to Tagori.

Arrow emerged from the stairs and began enchanting and firing arrows as fast as he could. Tagori couldn't tell whether he shot three or four, but each hit its mark. He activated them, saying, "Kon Kon." Instead of bursting, the blast set Icharro on fire. The trail of blood spilling from Icharro also burned, like a fuse on a powder keg. Slowly he burned and fell lifelessly to the ground.

Tagori ran to Tarin. The cut he had received looked bad, but Tagori had never seen war, so he had no idea what condition Tarin was in.

"Take him to Dago. He should be able to help," Arrow said.

"Emrila, you need to take him. He'll die before we reach Dago," Tagori said.

"Yes, I'll move as fast as I am able," she said, reaching her head down into the room.

Emrila grabbed Tarin's clothes in her jaw and lifted him out of the room. The room shuddered as she flew off to find Dago.

"We'll meet him there. Now let's go before anything else happens here," Arrow said.

As soon as they exited the tower, they could see Emrila flying away. They chased her. They didn't stop running until they reached the camp.

"I've done what I can, and the other two aren't in any condition to help right now," Dago said.

Verag and Enro were asleep already. Tagori forgave them because of the amount of drugs that were probably in their systems.

Tarin lay still. His face was still covered, though his shirt had been removed and was by the fire, where it was drying after being dampened by dragon saliva.

Tagori reached up to pull the cloth off Tarin's face.

"No," Arrow said, grabbing Tagori's wrist, "it's best you don't see that."

Tagori retracted his hand.

"Why can't I do anything? I bring disaster wherever I go," he told Emrila.

"I don't believe that. This would have happened regardless, though if you would not have been there, he would already be dead."

"I just wish there was something I could do."

"As do I, Tagori. As do I."

Tagori's hands began to glow. He looked at them for a moment before he knew what to do. He moved to Tarin and placed his hand on the bandage on Tarin's side. In an instant, Tagori pulled the bandage away while simultaneously grabbing the wound with his other hand. Tagori's right hand speared into Tarin's side, making him cringe in his sleep. He slowly pulled his hand out of Tarin's side as he felt the muscle and tissue regrowing around his fingers. When Tagori's fingers pulled free, he saw that the cut had already sealed shut, leaving only a faint scar.

Tarin opened his eyes and stared at Tagori's still glowing hands. He fell back asleep as the glow faded from Tagori's hands.

"What did you just do?" Arrow asked.

"I don't … know," Tagori said, struggling to get the words out.

"You didn't use words. How did you cast that spell?"

"That wasn't a spell—at least I don't think so," Tagori said.

"I've heard that tamers have some strange abilities; you must have used one," Arrow said.

"Everyone else is asleep, I think we should do the same," Dago said. "In the morning, we can figure out what happened."

Taking Dago's suggestion, Tagori lay down next to Emrila while Arrow and Dago checked on the other three to make sure they were still all right.

"Do you know what happened?" Tagori asked Emrila.

"No, but emotions are powerful. Remember that. It will be useful if you ever hope to do something like that again."

"Why do I feel as if you always know more than you tell?"

"I don't know. My words are true. It's up to you how to interpret them." She lay down to sleep.

Tagori watched the sun set as he tried to fall asleep, but he failed until the moon had replaced the sun in the sky.

He woke in the morning to find Tarin cooking what seemed to be a rabbit over the fire.

"Tarin," Tagori said, "I'm sorry."

"What for?"

"If I wouldn't have gone into that tower, you wouldn't have gotten hurt."

"Enro might have been killed before we got to him. If that were the case, we would have still ended up fighting that man. Chances are that

I would have ended up in that state anyway. Also, it's because of you that I am alive right now. Enro owes you his life as well."

They ate quickly, though Tarin ate away from the group. As soon as they were done, they decided to get back on the path to the Gilrund, which didn't take too long to reach.

"There it is, Tagori, the Gilrund," Arrow said, pointing at the magnificence of the Great Waterfall.

"Where?" Tagori said, seeing nothing. "Are you trying to tell me that this has all been for nothing?"

"Where would the Gilrund be if it weren't hidden?" Arrow said. "You shouldn't believe everything your eyes tell you."

They continued to the base of the falls, and Tagori realized what they were trying to tell him. The falls were hiding the entrance to the Gilrund. A cave large enough for Emrila to get through was hiding at the center of the falls, but how they were going to get there still eluded Tagori, for the water seemed deep.

Tarin urged them forward and stepped out, but he did not fall more than a few inches. Tagori found the thought of a submerged land bridge incredible.

"Now that we know the location of the Gilrund, we can report it back to King Venaran," Enro said.

"What?" Dago said, stunned.

Enro and Verag jumped into the river and began to swim away.

"Aberda Quanzel," said a soft, strange voice, the likes of which Tagori had never heard.

The water that surrounded them came up into a pillar that contained the traitors in the center.

"Great work, Cerrum," Arrow said without turning around. He seemed to know this person by voice.

Tagori recognized that name from somewhere but couldn't recall where. Then it hit him. Roz! This was Roz's boss?

"Let's take these two inside," she said.

The Gilrund! What an amazing place this was. The buildings were built out of the rock walls. There was a large hole in the top of the cave, covered with glass or magic—Tagori couldn't determine which. Through it, Tagori could see the water of the lake above them. Ledges jutted out of the wall on the way up to where the water was contained.

Enro and Verag were thrown into a cell and forced to drink a drug to seal their magical abilities again. When they were in the central chamber, they sat down and had a drink. Tagori was the first to break the silence.

"Cerrum, would you happen to know my brother, Roz?" he asked, still looking at her with a stunned expression. Cerrum was just as tall as Tagori was. She wore a blue dress and had pinned her long blonde hair back. Her form was definitely that of a woman.

"No ... no, I don't. Should I?" she said.

"I guess not," he replied.

"The reason we are here is because of Tagori," Tarin said uneasily.

"So the tamer decided to join us, then?" Cerrum asked.

"Well ... we kind of held his hand on the way here," Tarin said.

"So it wasn't his choice to be here?" she asked. "Well, then I guess he must decide now; tamer, will you join our forces?"

After all that Tagori had gone through, they gave him an option now? What would happen to him if he decided not to join them? He knew too much just to simply forget about him, although the Gilrund—or rather, those he knew in it—had protected him through their journey.

Tagori's mind was already made up. "I will," he said.

Cerrum smiled at his answer. "Good!" she said. "What of his skills?"

"Minimal in both weapons and magic. He needs someone to train him," Tarin said.

"All right, I'll find someone for him."

"I think you should know a few things about him, though. First, his sword is Zak'reen; second, he has managed to modify a spell, something you need to see."

"Really?" she said, her voice full of intrigue. "Let's have him demonstrate."

They walked through the hidden city to a small arena that was near the back of this cave.

"Let's see this spell he has made his own."

Tagori held his hand out in front of him. He grabbed the flow of magic he knew and spoke the word "Guinarun," making the air swirl and condense in front of his hand. In a matter of moments, the familiar ball of air hovered just inches from his hand. He moved to show that it followed him.

"Well, you really have made this spell your own," Cerrum stated. "I would imagine it would take anyone else quite some time to string together the words to make this possible."

"Do you have any idea why this would have happened?" Arrow asked, "We can't think of any reasonable explanation."

"I have heard that elements treat some people differently, but this seems to be on a completely different level. Has any use come of it?"

"It does a good job in battles," Tagori said.

"It redirected a thrown sword," Tarin said.

"Such strength from it? The air currents must be strong. What of your magic energy? Do you have headaches after sustaining it? How long could you keep it going?"

"I don't know how long I could sustain it."

"Which Zak'reen did he find?" she asked Arrow.

"All of them," he said matter-of-factly.

"What?"

"Just watch. Show her, Tagori."

Tagori released his hold on the magic, and the air dissipated, refreshing him. He then drew his sword and held it out in front of him. He commanded it to change into a spear, and the blade contorted, as did the hilt, until it was a six-foot-long spear.

"Amazing. Where did you find it?" she asked.

"The shrine hidden near Norico," Tarin said.

"That was the sword that was there?" she said. "Why was he able to pull it out?"

"Who knows? Maybe it just reacted because he's a tamer."

"It would have had to have an elaborate charm around it to prevent all but tamers," Cerrum said. "Although … there is something that you should look at."

"I would like to tell you one more thing about him, though I will find you later to do so," Arrow said.

She acknowledged this and led Tagori to a large temple, a place for the people to pray to whatever gods may worship. The stained glass in the interior made the chamber seem to be painted in some unnatural and beautiful color. She led him to a side room at the front. It contained little more than a flight of stairs leading down. The stairs opened up to a chamber that had a small altar, much like the one Tagori's sword had rested on, though on this one was a ball of silver chain.

"This is a special chain. What it is for, no one is sure. We have been unable to move it, but I feel as if you may be able to," she explained.

"Why do you think I'll be able to do anything?"

"Your sword was the same way," she said. "We have known about that shrine for quite some time, and a few have tried to take the sword. Obviously, none have succeeded until you were able to claim the sword. That is what makes me think you will be able to discern the use of this chain."

"What do you think I should do?"

"The exact thing you did when you took the sword."

"I didn't do anything special. I just grabbed it."

Cerrum looked at him, her expression confused. Tagori put his hand on the chain, waiting for something to happen, though nothing did. He closed his hands around it, his fingers digging into the metal links, and he pulled. It stayed still, as though the position it was in now were its permanent location in the world and nothing would be able to change that. After a moment, Tagori gave up.

She looked at the chain disappointedly. She seemed disappointed he was unable to do anything about the chain. Together they left the temple, and she led him to a second-floor room with a wall nearly completely removed. A curtain was all that separated the room from a small balcony.

"This will be your room. Emrila should have enough space to land on the balcony and join you in here. I have a few matters that need my attention, so if you would excuse me," Cerrum said with a slight bow.

She left the room, leaving Tagori completely alone. This room was furnished simply, containing only a bed and a small dresser. Emrila popped her head through the curtain and stared at Tagori. He lay on the bed and thought of how he used to do the same at his home, just lying there thinking that nothing would ever change. Now he knew how wrong he was. Nothing would ever be the same again.

"Emrila, I'm going to go look around," Tagori told her.

"Very well. I shall get some rest," Emrila said, roaring a yawn.

Tagori had no idea how long he wandered around the hidden city. He met so many people doing so that he simply didn't care about the time. Most everyone seemed to be so caring toward everyone else, helping others with their daily tasks or simply giving them a friendly smile and wave. Tagori knew that all the people here had lost something because of the empire, yet they all seemed to act as though they had not. How many people were hiding in here because the empire was hunting them? How many of those people were wrongly accused of their crimes? Tagori began to see the evil that the empire was capable of.

His wandering led him to the holding cell where Dago and Verag were kept.

"Why were you going to tell the empire where the Gilrund was?" Tagori asked, wanting to know if they should have been allowed to escape.

"We could've been killed by the soldiers that caught us," Dago told him. "But instead they made us a deal: if we told them the location of the Gilrund, then King Venaran would give us eternal life."

"But is that enough to betray your friends? What is the point of living forever if you regret every second of your life?" Tagori said.

Tagori turned to continue his exploration of the underground city.

Tagori soon ran into Cerrum. "Tagori, could you come with me?" she asked him.

Together they went to a library with skillfully painted glass windows. Light poured through them, illuminating all the books. The tables were crafted out of mahogany, Tagori noted. On one table, many books were opened.

"I heard about how you healed Tarin, and I thought I'd look into it," she explained. "You used a secret art that only a few tamers have been able to use."

"How does it work?" Tagori asked.

"It says here," she said, pointing at a book, "that you and your dragon must be feeling the same thing. In your case, it was sadness. But there is one strange thing about this: the more I look into it, the more questions I get. There is one thing that needs to be answered first. What makes this skill work? I mean, what is the energy that drives it?"

"So you want me to research this for you?" Tagori asked.

"Exactly," she said.

"I don't know how I can, though," Tagori said.

"All you have to do is describe how you feel while using it," she told him. "Right now, you have to go to training. If you have nothing else to do, you should go to the arena now."

When he arrived, a man wearing a brown cloak greeted him. "Ah, so you have come. I am Gebru. Let's get you started on sword training. Put this blindfold on."

"What?" Tagori exclaimed, confused.

"Oh, don't worry. I'll use this training sword so I don't hurt you," he said. "What you have to do, is parry my attacks."

Tagori did as he was told. Tagori heard footsteps, but he couldn't tell where they were coming from.

"Block now," Gebru said. Tagori didn't have any time to react before he was hit. "You need to get faster." And he did. Slowly Tagori parried most of his attacks. "Good. Now you must listen to where I come from. Tagori couldn't figure out how he could block the attacks. After what seemed like hours, Tagori heard the rocks crumble under Gebru's feet. He had a hard time figuring out where he was, so he took a chance but failed to block Gebru's attack. Tagori realized that sound was how he would figure out where to block. Another hour or so passed, and Tagori became increasingly better at blocking.

"Take off your blindfold," Gebru said. Tagori did as he was told. "We may now start on the spells. The first is Guinarega. It is a burst of air. Tezbiruo!" He made a target out of earth.

Tagori said the spell, and out of his hand shot a burst of air. The air hit the ground next to Tagori. He tried it once more, only this time he had his hand pointed at the target. It hit, making a hole in it.

"Good. There is a spell that could be a bit dangerous. It is Ginare Kantherk. When you say the spell, you must push your hands out when you finish saying it. If you do it too soon, it won't have much power, but if you do it too late, it won't move out very much," he told Tagori. "Are you up for trying it?" Tagori nodded. "When I say a spell, you use that one."

"Tezbiro Mendta!" Many of the stone targets came out of the ground and jumped at Tagori. "Ginare Kanthrek," Tagori said. When he finished his spell he thrust his arms out; Tagori could hear the wind howl as it made the targets crumble.

"Tagori, that was perfect!" Gebru said. "The basis of all wind spells is the word Guinar. All you have to do is combine that with any other word that you know; that should make it happen."

"Could we stop with the spells? Everything you have done has exhausted me," Tagori said.

"Yes, you have made more progress in one day than most of my pupils make in three," Gebru said.

Tagori and Gebru trained for hours. When Tagori's body was sore, they would train in the ways of magic, and when his mind was weak, they battled. There was so much on Tagori's mind that he had a hard time focusing on what they were doing.

"Tagori, what are you thinking about? Is it that chain?" Emrila said.

"Yes, I'm starting to wonder what it was made for. Who used it? How does it choose its owner? Even though we can use Dream Spark, it stays locked. But why? Maybe there's more to Dream Spark than we know."

"There's always something new to learn, but some things can't be taught by words. We must find things out on our own," Emrila told him.

Tagori was hit by many sword strikes while they were talking. Gebru stopped to ask what Tagori was thinking about. Tagori told him, but Gebru had no answers. He told Tagori that they were done for the day, and Tagori went back to his dwellings. He couldn't stop thinking about that chain.

Tagori had never had such a hard time going to sleep, but eventually he did.

V

Tagori awoke and saw that Tarin was talking to Emrila.

"Tagori, you're awake," Tarin said. "Verag and Enro's trial will start soon. You need to be there as a witness."

Tagori got dressed and went where Tarin had instructed him to go. The court was large, with a dome of stained glass.

"Verag, Enro, why did you want to betray us?" Cerrum said, seated in the judge's chair.

"We wished for eternal life," Enro said.

"How would you get eternal life?" Cerrum asked.

"The king would give it to us," Verag said.

"Why did you think King Venaran would give you eternal life?"

"All the guards said that if we told them the location of the Gilrund, the king would grant us eternal life," Verag said.

"Is that why you were talking to the guards outside of Areno?" Arrow said.

"How did you know about that?" Enro said.

"I thought that I saw you talking to the guards, so I used magnify sight, Gebedoken, and I was right," said Arrow. "I thought that they had just captured you and that you were begging to be set free."

"Did you actually think that the king could give you eternal life?" asked Cerrum. "Do you really think that he is that kind? If he could grant eternal life, don't you think that he would have made himself immortal by now?"

Tagori could tell that Verag was trying to think of a logical way to answer that question.

"Look, you two, the king has changed," Cerrum told them, "but he hasn't changed enough to take death away from someone."

"It is possible! All you need to do is string together the right words!" Dago said, becoming angry.

"But the mental strain would be incredible. The king would have to know everything in the world ... and more!" Cerrum explained. "If he had that much mental strength, don't you think that he would be doing the fighting himself?"

"No. He likes to see bloodshed," Enro said.

41

"Then don't you think that he would be there to see it?" Cerrum said.

What Cerrum had said must have had some truth, for Enro and Verag said nothing. They clearly couldn't think of a way to bring reason to their action.

"Enro, is it even worth betraying your friends and brother?" Tarin said.

"It's funny that you should say that!" Enro said.

Tagori looked at Tarin, trying to figure out what Enro meant by that.

"We apologize for the crimes that we have committed against the Gilrund," Enro said, speaking for the two of them.

"We could have you two executed. You're lucky that Dago doesn't want to see his brother die just yet," Cerrum said. "We will watch you closely, and if you step out of line, then we will have no choice but to put you in prison."

"Thank you, Cerrum," Enro said with his head bowed.

They all left the courthouse. Tagori went with Tarin to the library, where Tarin gave Tagori some books about great wind masters. Tagori read about the first person to use the wind to jump to his dragon, flying in the air far above him, and the person that used it to walk across the Grand River. He learned that both left themselves to the wind when they died. Tagori didn't understand what that meant, but he thought that it had something to do with their strong bond with the wind.

"Tarin, what spell did he use to—" Tagori was interrupted by a strange sound, almost as if the source were injured.

"Come … to … me …," the voice said.

"Tagori, what spell did who use?" Tarin said. It was as if he'd heard nothing.

"Did you hear that voice?" Tagori asked him.

"No, all I heard was you," Tarin said. "Tagori, are you all right?"

"Yes, I'm fine," Tagori said, not believing himself.

"*You heard it, right, Emrila?*" he then asked.

"*Yes, but as for who, or what, it is, I do not know. Where does it want us to go?*" Emrila said.

"*I don't know, but I think we'll find out sooner or later,*" Tagori said.

He turned to Tarin. "Tarin, I think I'm going to go back to my room."

"Right. I'll try to find some more books that could be useful to you," Tarin said.

Tagori left the library. He didn't really have a plan as for where to go, so he just wandered around. Tagori just couldn't believe what was happening: leaving home, his father and brother dying, and jumping into a war. Tagori then went to his room.

"*Emrila, let's go up to one of those ledges, the ledge under the water dome,*" Tagori said, more of a question than a command.

"*What for, Tagori?*" Emrila asked.

"*I just need to think,*" he told her.

"*About what?*"

"*Everything that has been happening over the past few weeks,*" he told her.

"*Right,*" she said.

Tagori jumped on her back, and she carried him to the ledge. The water was clear, and the sun shone through it. Tagori and Emrila talked about everything that happened since Tagori found the egg (or the egg found him), including the fact that Tagori's house was destroyed and his father and brother killed. Tagori had no family left except for Emrila.

Eventually Emrila and Tagori came down. Cerrum was running toward them.

"Tagori, we have a mission for you. Follow me to the courtroom," she told him.

"How did you know where to find me?" Tagori asked.

"It's kind of hard not to know when you have with you the only creature able to fly," she said.

Emrila growled.

"But how did you know I would be with her?" Tagori said.

"Well, it was just a good guess," Cerrum said.

The three of them went to the courtroom. Inside, Tarin, Arrow, Dago, Enro, and Verag were already waiting for the briefing.

"He's coming also?" Tarin asked.

"Yes, do you have a problem with that?" Cerrum asked him, not waiting for a response. "We need to locate a missing comrade. His name is Kaiben. He lives in a village southeast of here. The seven of us have been chosen to go see if he is all right."

"What if he isn't there?" Tarin asked.

"Then we have cause to worry," she said.

"Let's get going," Arrow said.

"We'll meet at the gate when you're ready to leave," Cerrum said.

They went to get their things. Tagori was eager to leave. He wanted to leave the dank setting of the cave. Tagori was the first one to the gate. Soon enough, Enro and Dago showed up. Dago had another brown cloak on, his arms covered by it. Enro had his ice pick on his back. Verag followed shortly, his hammer showing from behind him. Arrow showed. His quiver was full of arrows, and he had a long sword by his side.

"Well, we're all here. Let's get going," Tarin said. Tagori hadn't noticed Tarin sitting on top of one of the walkways.

"Cerrum isn't here," Arrow said. "Why do you not want her to come along?"

"She's one of the leaders of the Gilrund. She has important business to do," Tarin said.

"She still needs to get out sometime," Arrow told him. "And don't forget that you and I are both leaders as well."

Cerrum rushed toward them with two spears on her back. They were unique and had larger blades, more like an ax. They began to leave the cave. Tagori took one last look at it before he turned and left. It wasn't long before they were on a trail around the mountains.

The mountains that they were traveling past were amazing. Many of the peaks were lost in the clouds. The peaks that Tagori could see were covered with snow. They towered for what seemed like miles above him.

"Tarin, did something happen with your brother?" Tagori asked.

After shooting Tagori a quick glance, he said, "What do you mean?"

"What was with that comment Enro made during the trial?"

"You don't need to know about that," was all Tarin said.

Tagori decided it was probably best to drop the subject, though Tarin's past did interest Tagori.

Three men stood on a ledge above the path Tagori's group was walking along. They jumped down, holding on to the rocks to prevent them from sliding down the side of the cliff too fast.

"Are you with the king?" the man in the center said.

The man was covered in black armor; the other two men's armor had purple trim on it. Their faces were covered by helms that only showed their eyes.

"What if we are?" Tarin asked.

"Then you must be taken care of," the man said, drawing his sword.

"Stay your blade. I am a leader of the Gilrund," Cerrum said.

"Are you now?"

"Aye, as am I," Arrow said.

"What would be the odds of meeting two of the Gilrund's leaders out here today?"

"Granted, the chance is low, but we can assure you that we are leaders," Arrow said.

"Fine, I shall believe you. Let's keep searching," the man said, jumping up the cliff.

"Wait! Who are you?" Cerrum asked.

The man continued to scale the face of the cliff, temporarily ignoring Cerrum's question. "My name is Argerig, and this is Echo," he finally answered. "And that," he said, pointing up the cliff, "is Shadow. If we meet again, just hope that we are on your side." The two of them jumped away.

Argerig had a hammer on his back. Echo's sword was unique, it began as a broadsword, but at the top, it curved into two hooks. The top of the sword curved smoothly; it didn't come to a point as most blades did.

Despite being sidetracked by Argerig, Echo, and Shadow, the trip through the mountains was rather short. Soon they came to the village where Kaiben lived.

"Well, the town isn't that big, so if we split up, we should be able to find him," Cerrum said. "Tarin, you take his house. The rest of us will explore the town."

They split up, each searching a different part of town. Cerrum was right; the town was small. Tagori covered his part of town in about twenty minutes.

Tagori turned around to go back to the meeting point. A woman standing there startled him. Her eyes were almost white, as if covered in smoke. She wore a long robe, and her black hair was hanging in front of her face, small coins hanging on the ends of it.

"I sense much trouble in you, young one," she said.

"What do you mean by that?" Tagori asked.

"The ones that you call friends will accuse you," she said. "Your lack of dreams will be your downfall, but know that you will not be forgotten."

Tagori was scared of this new prophecy. He was going to die? How was he going to die? Tagori had so many questions but was afraid to ask.

Tagori ran to where the group was to meet. Dago was already there.

"Tagori," Dago asked, "is something wrong? You look scared."

"It's … nothing … Nothing at all," Tagori said.

One by one, the group returned, but still no Kaiben.

"This isn't good," Cerrum said. "He knew he was supposed to check in."

"Maybe something happened to the messenger bird," Arrow said in an attempt to calm her down.

"If it did, then we have a whole new set of problems."

"It's a small village. Are you sure that no one has seen him?" Tagori asked.

"We have asked everyone it's safe to ask."

"Let's head back. He may have been on his way; we could have missed him," Arrow said.

"Okay, we can only hope," Cerrum said.

They left the town, taking the same road through the mountains. Cerrum continuously glanced behind to see if Kaiben was approaching, though he never appeared. A few hours into their travels they arrived at a large flat and rocky outcropping. Yelling could be heard echoing from the stones. Everyone drew their weapons, and Tagori followed suit when he noticed the others.

From the other side, many men in silver armor came from the hill. Arrow already had an enchanted arrow ready. An arrow hit the ground in front of Tarin, and they looked up at the ledge. Archers had their bows pointed at them. Arrow turned to the archers and loosed his arrow, followed by a few more in rapid succession. Each hit its mark, either the head or chest of the archers. Arrow put his bow away, as he could tell that it wasn't going to be of much use to them with the archers out of the way. He then drew his long sword. The soldiers came running toward them.

Soldiers surrounded Tagori immediately, separating him from his companions. He was worried; he had never been in a battle like this. Tagori listened to the sounds around him. Did their feet make a different noise when they lunged to attack? He focused on the sounds the shuffling of feet made. Something changed behind him. He turned, bringing his blade up to block. The swords collided and bounced off each other. Tagori brought his blade around, using the force of the impact to strengthen his attack on a soldier on the other side of him, cutting past the chain mail he wore. He drew the blade straight back, pulling it from the man and hitting another in the head with his hilt. He swung his blade in a wide arc, scaring away a number of soldiers around him. A chance blow cut into Tagori's side, though only just.

Tagori scared away the soldier, giving himself some room. He held his hands close together, speaking the words "Ginare Kanthrek." As the last syllable escaped his lips, he dropped his sword and thrust his hands out, causing a shock wave of air to burst outward. Bodies flew in every direction, landing on other soldiers and even being flung down the side of the mountain. In the confusion his spell caused, he summoned the air orb that had already helped him in a few battles. A few soldiers had approached, but before they could manage a swing at Tagori, they tripped.

It took Tagori a bit to see the vines that were growing rapidly around their ankles. From behind Tagori, a man said, "I thought you could use some help."

Tagori was startled by this. He jumped and pointed the orb at him. "It's okay. I'm with the Gilrund," he said, "My name is Kaiben."

"You're Kaiben!" Tagori said.

Cerrum looked to see what Tagori was yelling about. As she did this, she was attacked from behind and hit squarely in the back by a hammer. Tagori saw this and threw up his arm, as if to catch Cerrum from falling. This sent the orb that Tagori was holding flying straight at the soldier that hit her. Once it hit him, it sent him spinning toward the cliff. The orb then returned to just above his hand.

Tagori grabbed his blade and ran over to Cerrum. Soldiers were quickly overtaking them. It took all of Tagori's skills just to keep the soldiers at bay. Once Kaiben began aiding Tagori, it was much easier to protect Cerrum. Tagori, while defended by Kaiben and his ax, dragged Cerrum's unconscious body to the wall. Tagori was holding the soldiers at bay and told Kaiben to go get some of the others and bring them to help protect Cerrum.

Only after Kaiben went to get the others, did the soldiers' skill truly show. They began to overtake him. Tagori thought he was finished. He saw the ax strike that would end it all, and he closed his eyes, expecting the worst.

A moment passed, and Tagori felt nothing. He opened his eyes. Fighting in front of him was Shadow, the man they had met earlier.

"Are they with you?" Shadow said sarcastically as he pushed the ax away.

Echo and Argerig were also aiding in the battle, and with them, soldiers were falling left and right, though their sheer numbers surprised Tagori.

He only got a glimpse of three Xen-Reths chanting something before a large glowing orb appeared. The orb shot up and then turned into a fireball. It came straight at Tagori. Emrila intercepted it and inhaled deeply. She opened her maw, releasing a great stream of flame, which collided with the fireball, causing it to stop. In moments, the fireball had dissipated, leaving Emrila breathing heavily. She spun and whipped a group of soldiers with her tail.

The Xen-Reths caused the battle to become more challenging. The spells they cast interfered slightly with the battlefield. Shadow and Nairu moved up to fight the Xen-Reths to prevent them from affecting the fights.

Echo told Verag to make walls around the battlefield. He told Verag to make them as flat as possible. Verag listened. Echo called everybody into the center of the battlefield. Kaiben and Tagori carried Cerrum.

When Echo cast the spell Edonri Myrthre, a large, strange bubble appeared. Echo told them all to go into the center of it. Without being told, Argerig and Shadow got about two feet across and cupped their hands. Echo began running toward them. Echo jumped and was caught in Shadow's and Argerig's hands. Together they pushed him up.

"Edonri Sevontra," Echo said. His hand became blurred in a strange purple light. Suddenly, Tagori saw cuts appear in the rock wall. Almost all the soldiers fell and convulsed for a reason that was unknown to Tagori. Only one person stood: Icharro.

"Arrow, look. It's that man from the tower Enro was in. How is he still alive?" Tagori asked.

"I don't know," he said.

"It doesn't matter. I'll take care of him with one spell," Enro said. He ran toward Icharro. "Secthoren Lachret," Enro said, and Icharro's arms froze in a block of ice. "Secthoren Lachrep" he said, making Icharro's legs freeze, "Secthoren Segartor," he said, freezing the rest of Icharro in a block of ice. "See, told you I'd take care of him."

Icharro broke out with little difficulty, and it seemed he wasted no energy at all. Enro ran from Icharro. Arrow told Kaiben to make three arrow shafts breakable at a certain point, just a little way from the head. He enchanted them.

"Enro, after I shoot him, I want you to use Ice Grave," Arrow said.

Arrow quickly fired all three arrows. Enro then cast the spells, encasing Icharro in a block of ice for a second time. Arrow yelled, "Kon Kon," and the arrows exploded. For a second, nothing happened. The ice shattered, making a large cloud of smoke. Once it cleared, they could see that Icharro was hurt but still alive! How could this be? A single arrow could blast a hole in a thick rock wall.

Icharro picked up a sword from the ground. He began to walk over to them as though he were unhurt, but it was clear that he could not run.

"Tagori, take one of Cerrum's spears and enchant it with the fire spell. Do you remember it?" Tarin asked.

"Yes, I think I do," Tagori said. He ran over and picked up one of her spears. "Erono Riorin," he said over it. It exploded into a fiery spear. Tagori gave it to Tarin, who already had his icy blade out.

"Dago, I need to strike the blades with lightning once they are embedded in Icharro's shoulders," Tarin told him.

Dago nodded. Tagori drew his own sword, saying, "You'll need help getting them in his shoulders."

They both ran, Tarin going right and Tagori going left. Icharro blocked Tarin's first strike with his own blade, which gave off a faint yellow glow. Tagori attacked but was blocked. This distracted Icharro enough for Tarin to stab him in the shoulders.

"Now, Dago!" Tarin yelled.

Dago began his spell as Icharro reached to take out the weapons. Dago finished the spell, and seemingly from nowhere, a bolt of lightning hit the hilts of the weapons. Icharro convulsed and fell to the ground.

Tarin cautiously walked over to Icharro and grabbed the weapons. He pulled the sword out easily, but he had difficulty with Cerrum's weapon. Silver blood poured out of the wounds. Icharro didn't move for a long time. Just as Tagori was beginning to think that they had won, he heard a laugh. The laugh sent a chill up his spine.

"Is that everything you can do? I fight opponents stronger than all of you for practice," Icharro said as he got up.

"What are you?" Arrow said.

"What am I?" Icharro said. "To you, I am your death!" He threw his sword into the group but missed everybody. "Zenta Sosari Rioki!" he yelled. Flames encased his body, though he didn't appear to be affected by them. The flames began moving, contorting into the shape of something.

"Everyone distract it," Tarin said. "It will take all his energy soon. Nobody is able to sustain that spell for long. If you get touched by it, you will surely die."

"Where have I heard that spell before?" Tagori asked Emrila.

"Is it not the same one Tarin used after you received your blade?"

"Is that how he defeated all those things that attacked us?"

"It must be."

The flame had become a giant serpent made only of fire. The snake looked around. It fixed its gaze on Tarin. The flame dove toward him, but Arrow pushed Tarin out of its way.

Tagori just stood in shock. He was trying to move, but his legs wouldn't let him. The snake dove for Tarin once more. Tagori's legs, moving on their own now, ran toward Tarin. There wasn't enough time to reach Tarin. Tagori had to do something quickly. Tagori said three words: "Zenta Sosari Guinari." The fiery snake stopped. The air began to be visible, just as it was with the Ginariun spell. Just like Icharro's spell, it was a snake. Tagori's and Icharro's snakes began to fight. Tagori, strangely enough, didn't feel tired or weakened at all. The Geth-zhan marks on Tagori's arms appeared and glowed brightly.

The wind snake began to eat the fiery snake, and soon there was nothing left of it. Tagori was shocked at this. He couldn't believe how strong the spell was. The snake looked at Icharro. He just stood there as if he planned to take it on himself. Tagori noticed that Icharro couldn't keep his balance. Could the effects of Icharro's spell be starting to affect him? Would this happen to him when his spell was finished?

"This is your target here!" said a voice that Tagori had never heard.

"Devour him!" another voice said. Tagori looked around and saw two shadowy figures near Icharro.

The wind snake let out a roar, and Icharro fell. The snake picked his body up in its mouth and crushed him.

As the snake started to crush Icharro, Tagori felt his energy begin to drain. A strange black fog flew from Icharro's body, which the snake then threw over the cliff.

The black fog flew around as though looking for something. It flew to the top of a cliff, straight to …

"Venaran!" Shadow yelled.

The three of them jumped up the cliff. When they reached the top, they drew their weapons. Shadow was quick to attack him. Venaran just threw his arm up and deflected Shadow's sword. He then spun around and punched Shadow in the stomach, making him fall to his knees. Echo and Argerig came running at Venaran, but he picked up Shadow and threw him at Echo and Argerig.

"You are growing, kid. All you need to do is harness the spark; then you might be able to beat me," said the king.

"What do you mean by that?" Tarin asked.

Venaran gave a slight laugh. "Let's just hope that you can find out," he said. Venaran slowly turned away. Shadow got up and ran at the king again, hoping to get an attack to connect with the king. Venaran turned around and picked up Shadow, throwing him over his head. Shadow landed on the ground with a loud hollow thud.

"I suggest you stay down this time," Venaran said.

The king just walked away.

"What did he mean by 'spark'?" Tagori asked.

"I don't know, but we'll have to figure out in order to kill him," Tarin said.

Cerrum opened her eyes, still dazed from the hit.

"Who were those people that appeared next to Icharro?" Tagori asked.

"I wonder if those are the people who gave themselves to the wind," Arrow said.

As they finished their journey back to the Gilrund with Cerrum riding of Emrila's back, Tagori couldn't stop thinking about what the king said. Harness the spark? What spark? The questions haunted him for the rest of the trip.

They arrived back at the Gilrund late at night. Cerrum was brought to her room as Kaiben went off to find one of the many medics. Tagori made his way back to his room, where Emrila soon joined him.

"Why do you torture yourself with these questions?" Emrila asked.

"*I need to know the answers to them.*"

"*But why?*"

"*The king killed my family.*"

"*And this will help bring them back?*"

"*No.*"

"*So stop thinking about it so much. Eventually the answers will reveal themselves.*"

"*All right,*" Tagori said, disappointed. "*Good night.*"

"*Good night, Tagori.*"

VI

Tagori woke well rested but sore from the previous night's battle. He needed to become stronger, strong enough to fight the king and win. He woke himself up and headed to the arena, finding it empty. He wanted to find Gebru to help him train. Cerrum should know how to find him. The problem now was how to find her. Tagori headed to the main library. He looked around a little before finding her at one of the many tables organized in the building. She had surrounded herself by many books of varying thickness.

"Tagori, I was just about to send for you," she said. "Tarin explained what happened at the pass, and I did a little research on the spark. I'm pretty sure the king meant the Dream Spark."

"I thought you didn't have anything about the Dream Spark."

"We didn't, but I told a few people to search for hidden areas, enchanted books, and anything that could be of any help. As it turns out, there was a room under a floor stone. A few bookshelves and gauntlets are under there, but it seems to be much like the chain that I showed you. Nobody can move it. You should go see the gauntlets if you have time."

"So what have you found?" Tagori asked.

"Well, you know that you have to be perfectly synchronized with your dragon, but it requires luck, skill, or great communication. Most tamers have only done it about three times in their entire lives. It is a very useful tool that can do anything. But," she said, "if you use it and then lose the synchronization, it can kill you."

"How?" Tagori asked.

"It can drain your reserves of energy," Cerrum told him.

"Oh! The reason I came here was to ask you if you knew where Gebru was," Tagori said.

"He went home for a while," Cerrum said. "Why do you want to know where he is?"

"I was hoping to start training," Tagori said.

"I'll train with you," she said.

The two of them went off to the arena. They decided to fight hand to hand for the first match. Tagori had never fought anybody, with the exception of his brother, hand to hand. Cerrum had to teach him many things, starting with the proper way to attack and ending with how to anticipate your opponent's attack. Tagori was not good at reading the attacks. All of their movements looked the same to him.

Arrow soon came to watch them fight. Cerrum seemed to have the upper hand in this fight, but she stopped to see if Arrow had anything to say. He did.

"The council has decided that we should go investigate how heavily guarded the king's castle is. If it's possible, try to take the king out of commission," Arrow said.

"So how are we going to go about this?" Cerrum asked.

"We will take a small team and go into the castle," Arrow said. "We will map out where soldiers and guards are stationed. We are going to try to make it so a large group can easily get to the king."

"Who will be in the squad?" she asked.

"Tagori, Tarin, Dago, Enro, Verag, Kaiben, you, and myself. Seems like a small enough group to keep defended and stay hidden at the same time," Arrow said.

"When do we leave?" Cerrum asked.

"As soon as we get everything we need," Arrow said.

"Why do I have to go?" Tagori said.

"Do you have anything else to do?" Arrow said. "And besides, we may have to fight the king, in which case your weapon could prove useful."

As Arrow and Cerrum went to the armory, Tagori stopped by the library and looked at the gauntlets that Cerrum told him about. They were dark silver-gray with white trim. An inscription was under the display, reading "Unlock."

Tagori then went to the armory, where Cerrum and Arrow were packing darts and a few other items that could prove to be useful. Everybody met there and soon headed out. The king's castle was close to the Gilrund. This was no accident, for if Venaran ever wanted to search for them, the last place that he would look would be close to his fortress. Sonnon wasn't very large; it took them only a day to see the great walls of the fortress. It was in a large open field. They could see it from the forest that was nearby. Since this was to be a stealth operation, they waited until dark to get near the castle.

The size of the castle shocked Tagori; he hadn't expected it to be so large. Tarin realized that they had no way of getting into the castle. They couldn't just knock on the doors. It wasn't as if the king's loyal men would let them in. They needed a way to get either over or under the wall.

"So what are you going to do?" said a deep voice that oddly sounded both friendly and commanding.

"I don't know. We will probably look for a weak point in the wall and try to—" Tarin was cut off.

"Why don't you just go under it?" the man said.

"Actually, we could go through it," Verag said, feeling the wall.

"Where does your allegiance lie?" Tarin asked.

"My allegiance is my own," the man said.

"Oh? You mean to say that you have yet to take a side?" Cerrum asked.

"Not necessarily. I have already decided against trusting the foolish king."

"If you are not with the king, then join us," Cerrum offered.

"I will consider your offer depending on how you fare inside. For the time being, I shall join you."

"What is your name?"

"I am called Nairu."

"I assume you are prepared for battle?"

"I would prefer to avoid conflict, but if I must, I will."

"Conflict may be unavoidable. Are you still willing to follow us?" Cerrum asked.

"What better way to observe?" Nairu replied.

"Verag, get us through the wall," she commanded.

Verag put his hand on the wall and whispered a spell. The stone seemed to flow as if it were a liquid, creating a hole right away. They stepped through into the courtyard. Looming overhead were many towers as colorless as the night sky. They knew that somewhere in one of those towers, the king lay in wait.

Arrow immediately dipped a dart in what Tagori could only think was poison.

"We want to try to not kill anybody so just use the sleeping potion, got it?" Tarin told Arrow.

"I'm one step ahead of you," Arrow said.

They stayed in the shadows of the towers, which worked just as far as the base as a large tower. Two soldiers were guarding the entrance. Tarin and Arrow each took out a long hollow tube and put a dart in it. In unison, they shot at the guards, who slapped their necks, looked around, and then passed out.

Arrow enchanted an arrow and shot it up in the tower, where it stuck. The purpose of this escaped Tagori, but he figured that Arrow must have had a plan.

"Okay, let's go," Tarin said.

The group moved to the tower as stealthily as possible. They tried to open the door, but it was locked. Verag volunteered to smash the door down, but Arrow wanted a way that would be less "deconstructive."

Cerrum stuck her spear into the door and pulled up, trying to push the lock off. They heard a sound. The door creaked open slowly when they pushed it.

The door led to a long hallway. Several doorways were on each side of it, leading into different rooms. They took the first door on their left. It led to a larger room with a table that was almost the same size as the room. On the opposite side were two doors, one up a small flight of stairs. They proceeded across the room cautiously. The top of the stairs seemed safe. They went into another large hallway. There were many rooms, perhaps for the guards to sleep in when they were off duty. At the other end of the hallway was a winding staircase. Stairs that fancy had to go somewhere important.

They reached the top and followed the hallway around until a small red and black door stood before them. Dago put his ear to it.

"Someone is inside," he said.

"How can you tell?" Tagori asked.

"I hear breathing," Dago told him.

They all drew their weapons, Arrow ready with an enchanted arrow, as always. Nairu had a pair of large claws. They looked like three small scythes on his hands. A strange series of ropes and pulleys made them able to move as though they were fingers.

They opened the door slowly. On the other side was a large room. King Venaran sat slumped in the throne. He wore black armor. Although the room was dimly lit, the armor glowed slightly brighter than the room. He rose.

"Welcome," Venaran said coldly. "I'm glad that you made it here. I assume that you didn't come here to talk, though."

"How right you are," Arrow said.

"Actually, if we could, we would try to persuade you to step down from the throne," Kaiben said.

"To do that, you must kill me. Put a scratch on me and I will think about it," Venaran said. He drew his sword. It appeared to give off a faint golden light, just as Icharro's did.

Tarin pointed his sword at the king and said, "I'll end you."

"I would like to see you try," Venaran said.

Arrow shot, making it blow up just before the king could deflect it. Arrow put his bow away and reached into a pouch. He took out small darts, enchanted them, and threw them past Kaiben, who was lashing at the king with his whip. None of the darts hit their mark; they were blocked by the king's sword. Cerrum, Tarin, Enro, and Tagori rushed the king. Tarin gave a slight nod, and Cerrum jumped at the king while Enro ran at him. The king spun and kicked Enro in the head. Tarin, who was now running at the king, dodged the kick. Cerrum was punched and slid as he hit the ground. Tarin's attack was blocked, and he was then picked up and thrown into Enro.

Tagori's Geth-zhan marks started glowing. He used the spell "Zenta Sosari Guinari." The beast appeared out of nowhere and lashed out at the king, who used his blade to cut the magic serpent in half, ending the spell.

"That's what I want to see, tamer. Use that power that you have," Venaran said.

The battle continued to rage on, with the king avoiding any damage and everyone else getting weaker by the second. Tagori knew the fight was pointless; the king had beaten Tagori's strongest spell with only one hand.

"Tarin!" Verag yelled. "Use a spell *now*!"

"Which one?" Tarin yelled back.

"Any!" Verag commanded. "Everybody else get behind him!"

Tarin began to mutter a spell quickly. Tagori ran to Cerrum, picked her up as best he could, and ran behind Tarin as fast as his legs would take him. Tarin finished his spell moments after Tagori had gotten behind him. The king sounded as though he finished a spell almost instantly after Tarin had. Light burst from Tarin, spreading in all directions. A purple ball shot from the king's palm. The ball continued to get larger but moved slowly, if at all, because of the effects of Tarin's spell.

"Good," Verag heard from behind him. "How did you know that I was using that kind of spell?"

"I saw your mouth say 'Negos,'" Verag said.

"You're very observant," Venaran said.

The king swung his arm around. Verag ducked and evaded the blow. He tried a leg sweep, but the king was unaffected by the attack. Venaran kicked up with his other leg. Verag rolled across the floor.

"If you were able to counter that last attack, then counter this," Venaran said. He pointed his arm at Verag and said, "Dark Erosion." A beam went straight at Verag.

Verag was thrown against the wall and was knocked out. Kaiben lashed at the king as Tagori went under the whip to grab Verag. Tagori ran with Verag over his shoulder.

"Kon Kon," Arrow said. The wall blew up. Arrow shot into the floor. He then shot across to another tower, closer to the ground. Connecting the two arrows was a rope.

"Everybody run!" Kaiben said.

Arrow took Verag off Tagori's shoulder and slid down the rope. Tagori was the last to go. He was watching Kaiben hold off the king, wondering if Kaiben would follow him. Tagori jumped and slid down the rope. Tagori joined the rest of them. Kaiben wasn't far behind him.

Before they reached the wall, an arrow hit the ground in front of their feet. Tagori looked up. On top of the wall were countless soldiers with arrows aimed at them.

"Stay where you are!" a commanding voice said.

"Tamer, stay with me and your friends can go safely," Venaran said from somewhere in front of the group. "If you choose not to, let's just say we'll have a few more targets for practice."

Tagori thought this over. The choice should be obvious: let all of them live. But was that what the rest of them wanted?

"I could cast a spell to reflect the arrows," Arrow whispered.

"With this many? No, it would hurt you too much," Cerrum said.

"Perhaps the combined strength of two or more?" Arrow said.

"No, they'll know that we are planning to use a spell, and they could continue the assault for a while, much longer then we could withstand, even if we were to all use the spell," Cerrum said.

"Maybe there is another kind of spell that we—"

"I'll stay!" Tagori interrupted, loud enough for everybody to hear.

The king smirked. "You know that by choosing to stay, you will have to be the one to bring down the Gilrund."

Tagori had not realized that he would have to follow the king's orders, almost become the king's fist!

"Do you still wish to stay?" Venaran asked.

"Yes!" Tagori said, clenching his fists.

"Good," Venaran laughed. "Now the rest of you be gone!"

"Tagori, you don't need to ...," Tarin began.

"Didn't you hear him?" Tagori said. "Get out of here while you still can! Take Verag to safety and tell Emrila to come here."

Tarin looked at Tagori as if trying to persuade him to come with them. The group ran off to the gate. Tarin took one last look back, wondering if they would ever meet on the same side of battle again. Tarin looked at Tagori, who just shrugged and gave a reassuring smile.

"Restrain him and throw him in the dungeon," the king said.

Tagori allowed them to bind his hands and escort him to the dungeon. They placed him inside a cell and left him to his thoughts. He had a rough time sleeping through the long night.

A large man in plain clothing woke him. The man roughly grabbed Tagori and led him out of the cell and into another room. The room had all sorts of painful-looking tools hanging on the walls. Many different devices also made their residence on the floor. He knew what was coming. He was given a sour-tasting mixture to drink, which quickly made him feel dizzy. His shirt was removed, and he was cuffed facing the wall.

"Tamer," the man said, "you need to swear your allegiance to the king, though your word alone isn't enough. We need to know that you understand the consequences for standing against him."

Tagori felt the lash of the whip against his back, the single thin tail cutting into his flesh. In unison, Tagori and Emrila, who could be heard from outside this windowless room, screamed out in pain.

The rest of the day was spent being tortured in various ways. When he was finally released, he was too sore to walk and was dragged back to his cell and thrown on the floor like a rag doll, bloodied and bruised.

"Emrila, what have I done?" he asked as he lay on the ground, barely able to move.

"You saved your friends' lives."

"Was it the right thing to do?"

"You are still alive, are you not?"

"That doesn't answer the question."

"Then perhaps you should ask it differently."

"Was it my place to save them?"

"You did what you thought you had to. In the heat of the moment, you took the most prudent course of action. All you can do now is endure what will follow. Stay strong. Things will work out."

"Even if it kills us?"

"Even if we are to die."

With that, Tagori tried to relax his sore muscles, and he eventually fell asleep.

Tagori was soon awakened and brought back to the chamber, where he was beaten and questioned for the vast majority of the day about the whereabouts of the Gilrund. Tagori accepted whatever punishment was dealt. After the sun had set, he was thrown back into his cell, barely able to move.

He heard some people talking outside his barred window after the second night.

"I tell you, the king dragon has him on edge," he said to his friend under his breath.

"It must, but can it even get out of the labyrinth? I heard it was supposed to be huge," the other said. No more could be understood from them as they walked away from his window.

"What do you make of that?"

"I don't know. Useless banter probably. "

Tagori's torture continued for three days.

"Em, I can't take this anymore."

"I know. So maybe you could give in."

"Are you crazy?"

"Not entirely. Look at it this way: if you give them the information they are looking for, then you can be in on the attack as well."

"So you are saying that I should trick them?"

"That is a simple way to put it. Certainly not the way I would say it, but yes, make them think that you are complying, though do so only to escape."

"You are aware of what can happen if this doesn't work out, aren't you?"

"I am. You will just need to play your part perfectly."

"I don't feel right gambling with their lives."

"I understand, but unfortunately, that is what has been happening since the Gilrund was created. Ever since you picked up the blade and ever since you decided to fight with the Gilrund ..."

"I hate it when you're right."

"I know, but everything will work out if you play your part well. Right now, you need to sleep and heal. You will need to steel yourself if you wish to perform well."

As usual, Tagori was awakened early the next morning. He was dragged into the same room and drugged. Once he was disheveled enough, he started to act on his plan.

"All right, I'll talk, though only to His Highness himself," Tagori said.

The two men looked at each other, and one signaled the other to leave, hopefully to get the king. It didn't take long for the man to return, allowing the king entrance.

"Have you had enough of this already, boy?"

Tagori looked up at the king through hair that was wet with blood and sweat. "The Gilrund," Tagori said breathlessly. "I'll tell you where they are."

"Then out with it!" the king snapped.

"The waterfall. They are under Origin Lake. The only entrance is under the waterfall."

"Is it now?"

"Yes."

"Good. You shall live knowing that you threw everything away for the greater good."

"Wait! Let me kill them."

"What?"

"They have left me here for dead. I won't forgive them."

"Hmm, we shall see." The king made his way to the door. Before exiting it, he said, "Get him cleaned up."

Tagori was thrown in the cell once again. After a quarter of an hour, two young maidens came in, washed him off, and bandaged his wounds. They left him, and he was locked in the cell alone once again.

"*What have I done?*"

"*It's all right, Tagori, Everything will work out. You just need to believe.*"

"*I know. It's just that what we are doing is so dangerous. We need to be correctly predicting what they will be doing.*"

"*You are right, but with what you said to the king, I'm sure that he wouldn't let the chance slip by to have the Gilrund be humiliated by a person they held to such esteem.*"

"*I wish I could warn Tarin.*"

"*I know. If I could get away, I would tell them myself, but there is nothing I can do either. We must just hope that they are able to defend themselves.*"

Tagori fell asleep unusually easy that night.

Tagori saw Tarin, but he looked like someone else. He was sitting on a hill outside of Norico. Tagori knew the town because he grew up there.

"Tarin?" Tagori said.

Tarin was shocked. He put his arm over his face and turned around. "Tagori!" he said.

"Tarin, I have to tell you about something terrible that I did," Tagori said regrettably. "I told the king where the Gilrund is."

"Why?" Tarin said.

"To gain his trust," Tagori said.

"How? Or more importantly, why?" Tarin asked.

"So I could come with the attack group," Tagori said.

"And help crush us?" Tarin said with some anger.

"I would fight on your side," Tagori said.

"Right," Tarin said in an angry tone that seemed more dismissive than anything. "Now, because of you, we have to prepare for battle!"

"I had to! If I told him later, then he would have less trust in me. He might not have let me come along! Please, Tarin, forgive me. I know that if I go along, we are sure to win."

"We'll see," was all Tarin said.

Tagori woke alone in the cell, cold stone walls on three sides of him and metal bars making up the fourth. Strangely enough, he wasn't tortured that day or the next.

The following day, Tagori was led outside, through the courtyard and to the armory. Tagori was given a simple set of armor and handed his sword. After he was equipped with everything, he was led back to the courtyard just in front of the main gate. Emrila waited at the other side of a large crowd of soldiers.

"Warriors," Venaran said, "soon we will make our stand against the Gilrund! We will crush all who thought they could stand against me! Against us!"

Tagori looked at the crowd of soldiers. Hundreds of people were standing and listening to the king. Tagori had a hard time believing that all those people were soldiers.

"You all know that you will be slaying traitors to the country, and I expect you to treat them like the scum that they are," continued the king. Now go—and allow the young tamer to be at the head of the battlefield."

They all turned to the gates, which were opened for them. As one, the army began to march out of the gates, at which point they turned to the east, heading straight for the Gilrund.

"Calm yourself Tagori; I can hear your heart beating from here."

"I know, but I can't. We have gotten one part of this plan completed. Now we just have to save the Gilrund from this massive army that we are a part of."

We may be a part of it now, but once the fighting actually starts, we will be able to surprise the soldiers and gain the upper hand."

"Yes, but it still involves fighting."

"I wish as much as you that we didn't have to fight, but unfortunately we must."

Tagori clenched his fists, causing some of his knuckles to pop. Today would decide if the country's fate could be changed.

The army reached the river and followed it north. Tagori stuck his nose out to fill his lungs with the river's scent. In the short time he had spent living with the Gilrund, he had gotten used to the smell of the damp air. In what seemed like no time at all, the waterfall was in sight. Tagori stopped to catch his breath, as he was nervous for the battle.

"Do you think they will be able to defend against this attack?"

"If they had prepared, maybe, but now I don't know. They may suffer heavy losses."

"I really hate the truth."

"What will you do?"

"No idea. I've been thinking it over for quite some time now."

"I know. Don't worry, you'll think of something."

Tagori led the army behind the waterfall, cursing himself for what he was doing. After a short walk down through the cave, he could see the small village that was the Gilrund. Lined up in front of him were the Gilrund's soldiers, ready for the assault already.

"Em, what does this mean?"

"It means luck is on our side."

"Tamer!" Cerrum yelled out. "Why have you betrayed us?"

"Silence yourself, leader of the Gilrund, or I shall silence you myself," Tagori replied. The words stung as they left his lips. "Each one of you is charged with treason. You have all sworn to kill the king at the cost of your own lives. The punishment for this is death. You see before you your executioners. What you do now is up to you. You can face us head-on or stand back and make this easier on yourselves. Should you choose the latter, I can assure you that this will be quick."

"What do we do?" Cerrum asked Tarin, who was standing beside her.

Tarin looked at Tagori. He knew that something Tagori said just wasn't right.

"What were those two choices he gave us?" Tarin replied.

"Face them or stand down."

"You sure he said to stand down? I heard 'stand back.'"

"What difference does it make?"

"I hope it means everything to him. I say we listen to him." Tarin turned to the Gilrund. "Brothers and sisters, hold the line. Do not let them take us here in our own home."

"If that is your choice, very good!" Tagori said, acknowledging the decision Tarin made. "Attack!"

The soldiers moved around him, swarming the Gilrund. Tagori put his hands in front of his body in a familiar position. Soldiers were rushing past both sides of him. He had to act quickly if he was to do any damage to the soldiers' morale.

Two words escaped Tagori's lips: "Ginare Kanthrek." Tagori's hands shot out as the last sound escaped. The spell was new to Tagori, but he used it as though he has been doing so for years. A bubble of air pushed outward, sending people flying in all directions.

Emrila flew over the action, and Tagori jumped to grab hold of her foot, managing to kick a few soldiers in the head as he flew over them. She dropped him off just outside the war zone so he could catch his breath and focus. From where Tagori stood, he could see Kaiben beating soldiers back with a whip he had made. He commanded the whip with great skill.

Tagori pushed through the front, trying to find Tarin. He found Tarin on the ground, surrounded by soldiers on one side and Gilrund on the other. Tagori ran full speed at the soldier that was about to cut Tarin down. Tagori jumped and rammed his shoulder into the soldier. He followed up with a spin kick and a stab with his sword.

"Thanks," Tarin said as Tagori helped him up.

"Did you know that we were coming?" Tagori asked him.

"I had an idea that you were," Tarin said.

"How?" Tagori asked him, trying to defend from oncoming attackers.

"You told me in a dream," Tarin said.

"Were you sitting on the hill near Norico?" Tagori asked.

"How did you know?" Tarin asked.

"I had the same dream," Tagori said.

Tagori and Tarin began to focus more on the battle than talking. The clang of the blades became a constant sound. The soldiers began to close in on the Gilrund, pushing them back. Tagori knew something had to be done before they were forced to surrender, for which Tagori would not be shown mercy. Tagori tried to think of a spell that he knew that would be of great usefulness. All the spells that Tagori had heard ran through his mind. Should he use Zenta Sosari Guinari? No, seeing as how Tagori couldn't control it, it would be too dangerous. He could not use Ginare Kanthrek; the people were too close. Edonri Sevontra …

"Tarin, do you remember that Echo used the spell 'Edonri Sevontra' in the battle? What does it mean?" Tagori asked.

"It means 'Blades of Sound.' Why do you ask?"

"Is there a spell for 'Gale Blades'?" Tagori asked.

As Tagori finished saying this, the blade of his sword began to glow as it did when it was changing. Why would it be changing? Tagori hadn't told it to change. The glowing blade became lighter in his hand. The blade was in the shape of an inverted angular U much like a standard sword, though a hollowed-out center held an extended hilt and a wire that was woven around others, making diamond patterns. In essence, it looked like two cleavers back to back. The sword was about four feet long. The hilt was about two feet, including the extra segment past the guard.

Tagori took a second to look at the new sword in awe. It felt incredibly light. Tagori was torn from looking at the sword when a soldier came slashing at him. He raised his arm to defend from the attack. The blade was so light that Tagori thought he had dropped it. Tagori pushed the enemy's blade away and with great speed, followed up with a slash to his shoulder. The guard fell to the ground writhing in pain.

Was this new blade Zak'reen's true form? Did the first owner of the sword know about this?

This blade, at this time, was a gift. This weapon would help him defend himself and others. This blade could save the Gilrund.

Tagori ran into the group of soldiers. Tagori moved his hand, and the blade appeared to defend its wielder. The blade moved smoothly through the air. Tagori could easily overpower anybody that he ran into. The soldiers realized that they couldn't overpower the Gilrund now that Tagori's new blade had given not just him but everybody around him renewed strength. Many more soldiers were falling to the power of the Gilrund.

Tagori had not noticed the Geth-zhan marks on his arms glowing strongly. Tagori muttered the spell Guinarega and a giant ball of air shot out, pushing down everyone in its path. Bodies went flying in every direction.

"Retreat, men! Retreat!" yelled the commander of the army.

All the soldiers that could move ran to the entrance of the Gilrund in order to retreat.

"Stop!" Tarin commanded.

All of the king's men were leaving the Gilrund. Tagori knew that the king would send more to attack, now that he knew where they were hiding.

Tagori walked back to the group of people. Many of them raised their weapons at him, knowing that only he could tell the king the location of the Gilrund.

"Lower your weapons. Tagori told the king our location, but he fought on our side," Arrow said, approaching him. "If we were to die, he would die as one of us. Welcome back."

"Thank you, Arrow," Tagori said, "but I do not deserve to be treated as a hero."

With his head lowered, Tagori, slipped off to his room. Emrila joined him after reacquainting herself with the place.

A long silence followed. The only sound was that of the waterfall, which could always be heard. Tagori had forgotten how good it sounded. The sound relaxed him into a deep sleep.

When he awoke, Emrila flew to him.

"Good morning," she said. *Did you sleep well?"*

"Yes," he said groggily. *"I'm sore all over."*

"That's what happens when you participate in a war."

"Did I really get hurt that much?" Tagori asked, looking himself over. *"Where did these bandages come from?"*

"Cerrum came by."

"So she did this?"

"She did. She was patched up herself."

Even after Tagori had betrayed their trust, Arrow had defended him and Cerrum had been kind enough to treat his wounds herself.

"Tagori, I've been thinking of the chain that Cerrum showed us a while ago," Emrila said. *"I think we need to try to unlock it again."*

"Why? What have we learned in the time between then and now?" Tagori said.

"We've learned plenty," Emrila said.

Tagori had no idea what Emrila had planned. Tagori followed Emrila to the familiar building where they had seen the chain for the first time. They went below to the altar that displayed the massive ball of chain. As they approached it, Tagori felt something different in the air. This unusual feeling made his stomach feel knotted up.

"So what do we need to do?" Tagori asked Emrila.

"What are you thinking right now?" she asked.

"*What?*" Tagori said. He thought long. "*I guess I'm wondering who will be the one to own this chain ... and what it's used for.*"

"*Focus on only that,*" Emrila said.

Tagori was confused but nonetheless did what she told him. Everything in his mind was put aside.

After a while, Emrila said, "*Tagori, tell the chain to unlock.*"

"*But what did this—*"

"*No questions,* Emrila interrupted. *Just do it.*"

"*Chain of the tamers, unlock!*" Tagori said.

They waited for a moment. Nothing happened.

Tagori sighed. "I wish that we ... I wish ... I wonder ... I wish the chain would unlock."

The sound of tumblers turning in a lock resounded throughout the room, quietly yet clearly audible.

Tagori looked at the chain again. It now was now moving, shrinking in size. Tagori reached out to touch it with his right hand. A wristband shot out of the moving ball of chain. It latched onto Tagori's wrist. The chain was moving into the metal band. He turned the band over to see the bottom of it. In the space between the metal, the chain was weaving in and out the sides. Once the chain was pulled in, a small claw stopped it. Once all the movement stopped, Tagori could finally examine the chain.

It was a metal band about three and a half inches long. The claw had three "fingers" that came to a squared edge. The tips of them were spaced about an inch apart. The brace was adorned with two small gems on each side. It fit on his arm perfectly, as though made for him.

Tagori emerged from the building, the bracelet glinting in the sunlight. He ran to find someone: Tarin, Cerrum, or another one of his friends. He stopped by Tarin's room and knocked on his door. After a short wait, Tagori turned to walk away, but the door opened behind him.

"Tagori, is something wrong?" Tarin said.

"Tarin, I was in the secret chamber where the chain was ... and this happened," Tagori said, showing Tarin the wristband.

"What is that?" Tarin asked.

"It's the chain. The one that was in that chamber," Tagori said.

"That was just an old ball of chain. How could that band come from it?" Tarin asked.

"I don't know. It must have been hidden in the center of it," Tagori said.

"How did you do it?" Tarin asked.

"I'm not sure. Emrila told me what to do, and it worked," Tagori said.

"We must go tell Cerrum," Tarin said.

"I was hoping I would run into her on my way here," Tagori said.

"I know where she is."

Tarin led Tagori to the central building. Inside were doors to many rooms, one of which was the courtroom. Tarin took him to the left and through the third door. On a desk in the room were many important-looking papers. Cerrum sat at the desk.

Tarin closed the door behind them, and Cerrum looked up.

"Tagori? Where did you get that wristband?" Cerrum said.

"From the secret chamber," Tagori said.

"What do you mean?" Cerrum said.

"This is the chain," Tagori replied, "the one that nobody could move."

"Impossible! There were hundreds of pounds of chain there, yet you wear it upon your wrist?" Cerrum said in disbelief.

"I don't know how it became light enough to wear," Tagori said, "but it seems that I was meant to have it."

"Tell me if you find anything new about it. I have some work that I need to get done, so if you would please excuse me," Cerrum said.

"Yes, indeed," Tarin said with a bow. He turned to leave; Tagori gave a slight bow and followed.

Tagori stopped before he left the room. He turned back to Cerrum. "Cerrum, do you know if Gebru is back yet?"

"No, it should be three months or so before he returns," Cerrum told him, clearly paying more attention to her work.

They quietly left the room.

"Emrila, let's go back up to the water," Tagori said to her.

Emrila flew to pick him up and then carried him to the rocky outcrop they called their own. Tagori sat on the edge and examined the chain that was now his—or perhaps it always was. He gave the claw a slight tug, but it wouldn't move. He looked at the city that was hidden away by the water. The city was large, although not many people lived there. Tagori could never go back to his home, for he had no other home.

"Emrila," Tagori said in a sad tone, "look at what the king has done to us. He pushed us back into this little hole. He made us be afraid. This is our world. *We* should control it."

"*Yes, Tagori, we should,*" Emrila said to him.

"I will defeat the king," Tagori said. "I will make Sonnon a safe place for everybody to live in. I swear it upon my life! I swear I will defeat the king!" He was now yelling loud enough for all to hear.

As Tagori turned around to lie next to Emrila, the rocks under his foot slipped away, bringing Tagori with them. Tagori began to fall to the city that lay only fifty feet below. Tagori was flailing his arms, and before he realized it, his arm was being pulled up. He thought Emrila had grabbed him. However, when he looked up, he saw that the chain attached to his arm had caught him. Five feet of chain was out, leaving Tagori dangling by the rock. Tagori used all his might to pull himself up the side of the rock.

"*Emrila, could you take me down?*" Tagori said, a little embarrassed.

"*Why? Is it too long of a drop?*" Emrila said jokingly.

When they landed, Enro came running up to them.

"We were sent to get some supplies. Would you like to come with?" Enro said.

"I'm going to look at a few things here … unless you really need me to help," Tagori said.

"We have a large team. We shouldn't need you, but it would be helpful if we had another pair of hands," Enro told him.

Tagori wanted to look in the library at the gauntlets that were hidden away, so he decided not to go along. Enro and Tagori said their good-byes, and Tagori headed off to the library. Emrila went out to hunt for some food.

Tagori removed the floor stone and jumped down into the room. The room was well lit for having no light source of its own. Tagori looked around and found that there were tiny mirrors lying around, reflecting the light in all directions, making the room brighter. He saw the armor lying on a pedestal, just as the chain had been. Tagori examined it but found nothing unique or out of place. There was no writing like on the one for the chain. However, the chain did feel a little heavier than normal. Something seemed familiar to Tagori, but he couldn't tell what it was. Tagori looked around the pedestal. There had to be something that made the armor able to move.

There was nothing for Tagori to do; it was not as if just looking at it would make it move. He left the chamber and sealed it up again. Tagori went to his room and picked up his sword. He was still surprised at how light it was. He decided to go to the arena for some practice.

Once in the arena, he swung it, remembering how it had appeared in his time of need. Was it just a coincidence that it happened? Was someone watching over him? The appearance of the sword raised too many questions. Maybe dear old Dad was watching over him from wherever he was. No. Tagori tried not to think about his father. The memory was too painful to endure once again.

The strange metal of the sword made it seem as though the sword disappeared when he swung it. His movements seemed more fluent than usual. The blade seemed to change part of him when it did. Tagori swung it around him as if he were in battle and about to cut someone down with it. The sword hit something and stopped. Tagori jumped back in surprise at seeing Tarin standing there holding Tagori's sword in the crescent blade of an old but sturdy-looking scythe.

Tagori's right arm flew to the side, and the chain shot out of it and into the wall of the arena. Tagori and Tarin looked at where the chain hit the wall, over twenty feet away. Tagori pulled his arm back and the chain, although tight, came free. Everything Tagori did caused new questions. Everything surprised him.

"What are you doing here?" Tarin asked.

"Wondering what's next," Tagori said with a solemn tone.

"What do you mean?" Tarin asked.

"We can't beat the king yet; we are not strong enough," Tagori told him. "How do we get stronger? What is there for us? How do we beat the king?"

"I don't know how we are going to beat the king, Tagori, but we must. The fight will be difficult, but we must prevail. He might be harder to kill then a tamer is," Tarin said. "I will leave you to your training." Tarin made some stone figures for Tagori to attack.

Tarin left Tagori to ponder the words he had just said. Tagori did think about the words, especially "harder than a tamer." Tagori remembered hearing something about a dragon other than his when he was trapped at the castle. Tagori ran back to the library to look for a map. He quickly found what he was looking for. He looked for any labyrinth that would be large enough to hold a dragon. Tagori had much difficulty finding this. Either it didn't exist or nobody knew it was there.

Tagori finally found one map that had it: the maze. No wonder no other map had it; it was far to the northeast, where no cities were. The Grand River didn't even go that far north. Tagori estimated that it would take about a day to get to the maze. It was a trip that they needed to take if they were to take out the king. Tagori remembered that if a tamer's dragon was killed, so was the tamer. Tagori believed that the king's dragon was there. Tagori gathered up the map and all the other tools he had been using and ran to Cerrum's office.

Cerrum was only about halfway through the stack of papers that she had been going through. Tagori sat down across from her, and she cleared off her desk, seeing that he had many papers. Tagori put them down and began to explain his plan to her.

"There is only one map that has this on it," Tagori began. "I'm sure that it exists, because the king is thinking about what's inside it."

"What exactly is inside it?" Cerrum asked.

"His dragon," Tagori said confidently. "The king is a tamer. If we could defeat his dragon, we could bring him down."

"That's a great plan!" Cerrum said. "How long does it take to get there?"

"I estimated about a day if we keep up a good pace," he told her.

"How many do you think it will take?"

"Only the usual team," Tagori said.

"We'll pack, and when Enro returns, we will set out. Tell the rest of the team," Cerrum told him.

They both left the room to find the teammates and to get supplies for the daylong trip. After Tagori found Tarin and Kaiben, he went to his room and packed some food. Tagori was sad that he had no more food from Norico to bring along; it seemed to give him more energy, if not pride. Tagori strapped his new sword to his back and eagerly waited for the moment they would leave.

Tagori took one last look around the Gilrund before leaving it for almost three days. He was saying good-bye to all the people that had become his friends—no, his family—during the past few months. When Tagori heard people heading to the gates to lend a hand to the group that had gone to get supplies, he went to tell Enro that they were going to leave for the maze.

Enro didn't seem surprised that they had figured out a plan in his absence. He went to pack and came back to see the rest of the group already assembled.

Enro stood there with his pickax sticking out from behind him in a menacing manor. Dago was hidden by another cloak. Tarin remained as mysterious as usual. Cerrum, although a little worried, stood there proudly. Kaiben was so excited that he couldn't stand still. Verag looked at the opening to the Gilrund. Nairu was examining his weapons, making minor adjustments to the new gear system that he had put in. Arrow stood proudly with his quiver full of arrows. Tagori could have sworn that he saw a small flame come out of it every few minutes. Using the ring he had taken from the remnants of his father's home, Tagori had his sword fastened to his back.

"Let's go. This could be the final battle of this pointless war," Tarin stated. The group of them set out to find a maze that could possibly not exist. They were going off pure trust.

They left the waterfall and headed to the east shore of the Grand River. They headed northeast, in the direction where the maze should be. They went into the forest that was kept alive by the fertile waters of the Grand River. The trees were thick, and many greens grew around there. They took their time eating all the wild berries they found hidden amongst the bushes, for after they left the forest, there would be no more water or food for a long time—only what they could carry on their backs.

The trees began to be smaller and the land less squishy. The forest was slowly disappearing and leaving only a desert. Soon sands could be seen as well. They decided to camp there until night, when the desert would be cooler. The hours passed, and Tagori hardly slept. He felt strange, as though they were forgetting something. Dusk set in, and they packed up the camp.

They were the first people to walk on the desert sands for more than one hundred years, and they continued the journey to the maze by the light of the full moon. They began talking about what they should do if they didn't find the maze by morning., deciding whether to turn back or continue.

Matthew Getzfred

They couldn't finish their "productive conversation" (fight is more accurate) for they found the maze standing alone in the desolate landscape. They couldn't tell how far away it was, but they knew it was there. The group quickened the pace to get to the maze faster and away from the rising temperatures of the desert. The doors to the maze became clear. Tagori was the first to lay his hands upon the door. The Geth-zhan marks on his arms glowed, revealing a strange symbol on the door. Nobody got a good look at it, for it faded from view soon after it appeared.

The doors opened with no problem. Once Tagori stepped inside, he could tell that something was wrong. An air of fear and worry hung stagnant in this place, left undisturbed for unknown years. The pathway was just big enough to let Emrila through. The path turned right and left for hours. Tagori lost track of how many miles they seemed to have walked. Around a corner, they came to a flight of stairs leading to a floor below them. Tagori was amazed at how well the building was constructed. It must have taken many years to create, especially with the high temperatures of the desert.

Many hours, or perhaps only minutes, of running led them all to a pair of large doors. The doors had exquisite designs on them. The feeling that Tagori had experienced when he first set foot in this place had only increased as he neared the door. The doors refused to open, and it took all of them and Emrila to push them open. On the other side of the doors was a large chamber about three stories tall. The room had a large pit on the other end of it. What was the pit for?

Tagori heard a familiar growl. "Did you hear that?" Tagori asked them, somewhat hoping this was where the dragon was.

"Yes," they said, almost in unison.

"You have finally come," the voice said. The voice was old, as though it had been there for many, many years. "Why have you come, though?"

"Did you hear that?" Tagori asked the rest of them. Tagori needed no reply; all the others grabbing their weapons was answer enough.

A giant golden claw grabbed the top of the pit, followed by another. The head and body of an enormous golden dragon come out of the pit.

"Are you the king's dragon?" Cerrum asked it.

"You disrespect me by saying that I am property?" the dragon said.

"Do you have any ties with the king?" Cerrum asked it.

"Yes," the dragon replied.

"We must defeat you!" Tarin said.

"You cannot hope to defeat me in the state you are in," it said. "I can only be beaten by the use of a spark."

"A spark?" Dago repeated. "How's this for a spark? Zesenrez." A bolt of lightning struck the dragon on the head, making it scream out in pain. The rest of the group ran to surround it. Tagori continued to run at the dragon, hoping to attack it while it was stunned. The Gale Blade swung down. Tagori felt it be deflected only moments before he was hit on the side. Tagori was sent spinning through the air and landed near the wall. Cerrum ran over to Tagori. Tarin jumped at the dragon's back but was hit away by the tail. Tagori got up and ran at the dragon again. Dago was using many electric spells, but they were having no effect.

Dago realized that it was pointless trying to zap the dragon, and he pulled out his broadsword. He lit the blade with electricity and slashed, knowing that the dragon would try to hit him. The sword plunged into the dragon's hide, only going as deep as the scales. Arrow was shooting arrows as fast as he could around its feet. Verag was trying to encase its feet in stone, and Enro was making pieces of ice shoot at the dragon.

Tagori tried to attack, this time calling upon his air orb to help him in the fight. Tagori saw the claw come toward him and jumped, using the orb to give him more height. Tagori just cleared the claw and was hit by the other, knocked straight to the ground. Tagori was trapped under the claw. The dragon looked down at Tagori and opened its mouth. Flames began to build up, and Tagori was prepared for the worst. Tagori suddenly fell into a hole. He saw the fire come, but it disappeared as the hole sealed itself up. Nairu had dug a hole, and Verag had sealed it up.

They ran to the far opening, for they knew that if the dragon found it, they would be burnt to a crisp. They emerged and began the assault again. Tagori knew that they could do nothing to win. He thought long and hard as the battle raged on around him. He decided to try one last spell. If it didn't work, nothing would.

"Zenta Sosari Guinari!" The great snake appeared, and Tagori hoped it was to aid him rather than harm his friends. The snake looked around at the victims it could take. When it saw the fire come from the dragon's mouth, it struck out at the dragon but was ripped apart by the dragon's great claws. The snake reformed and attacked again. It hit its mark, latching onto the dragon's throat. It bit hard but couldn't pierce the hide of the dragon. In the meantime, the dragon had seen the magic connecting the snake to Tagori. The dragon took aim at Tagori, who stepped aside to avoid the blow. The magic connecting them was caught by the fire and ignited.

A bubble of fire went up around Tagori. He could only see glimpses of the snake being incinerated by the fire. The fatigue then hit Tagori, and the fire bubble faded away. Arrow ran to Tagori to get him to safety.

"Tagori, are you all right?" Arrow asked him. "Your magic burned. Normal fire can't burn magic."

"Dragons don't use normal fire, do they?" Tagori said as he stood up. His sword was at the ready and the air orb found its way back to his hand. Tagori ran at the dragon once more. Tarin was attacking its left side and Cerrum was focusing on its right. Tagori ran under it, only to be grabbed by its tail and thrown against the wall behind it, the same wall with a deep dark hole below it. Tagori fell down that hole, out of everybody else's view.

Tarin screamed out Tagori's name as the dragon hit him with its claw. Everybody looked at the hole. Nothing moved. Rage filled everybody's eyes. They ran at the dragon, who whipped and attacked them. Tarin used his greater spells. The dragon just brushed off the spells as though nothing had happened. The dragon's tail whipped up to strike underneath it, and Tagori was flung into the air, the chain on his wrist retracting as it extended. As he descended toward the dragon's head, he thrust his sword down, hoping to cut the dragon at last. The blade managed to cut past the scales. Tagori was thrown off the head by its excessive shaking. He landed on the ground and rolled toward Emrila.

"Emrila, throw me with your tail, just like that," Tagori said aloud.

Emrila nodded, and Tagori grabbed her tail. She spun around to get more momentum. Tagori flew toward the dragon. The gold dragon saw Tagori through the distractions around him and blew a flame at him. The fire hit him and stopped him in the air. Tagori went straight down and hit the ground headfirst. The dragon reared up to crush Tagori in his maw. The dragon descended but was stopped by Emrila, who bit the dragon's neck. The dragon reeled in pain and hit Tagori with his claw. Tagori flew and hit Emrila. Emrila took her mouth off the dragon's neck and looked at Tagori. The dragon pushed Emrila out of the way.

Tagori stood up, saying, "I may fall, but my friends and I have enough courage to stand up again. We will defeat the king at any cost."

The dragon shot Tagori with a fireball. Tagori had never imagined that feeling such pain was possible. His skin was burning from the strange flames that dragons use. He went to his knees.

"Looks like there's no going back for me, huh, Emrila?" Tagori said. "I guess I've used you enough, wind. It's now time for me to give back to you. Wind, I give my body up to you." Tagori fell forward. His body began to become one with the wind.

"*No, Tag!*" Tarin screamed.

Only one person had ever called him Tag.

"Brother!" Tarin said as he pulled off his face mask, revealing the familiar face of Tagori's brother, Roz. Roz ran out to Tagori and grabbed him just before he hit the ground. "Tag, I'm sorry. I should have told you."

"Now's your chance to run," Tagori said breathlessly. "I'll see you on the other side."

"No, Tagori! Don't say that!" Roz said.

Tagori's body disappeared into the wind.

"*No!*" Roz screamed at the top of his lungs.

An explosion of air came from in front of Roz. It was strong enough to push the dragon back into the pit and everybody else out of the chamber. The doors slammed shut, and Tagori's sword was lying in front of it. Emrila picked it up in her teeth, and they left the maze. The trip back to the Gilrund was long and silent. Roz may have been spoken to, but he didn't hear anything.

Although there was no body, Tagori's funeral was arranged. A funeral pyre was set up to honor the fallen tamer. Tagori was recognized as many things during his funeral, none of which was tamer. He was called much more honorable words: hero, friend—and brother.

With glazed-over eyes, Roz looked at the fire that was made for his brother. Roz just stood there and let a tear roll down his cheek. A slight wind blew in his face as if to wipe away the tears. The family that Tagori had thought he had lost was now truly fading away for Roz. Two had already died. How long would it be before the king took the third away from him? The fire burned on to remember the one that had touched the hearts of so many in such a short time.

It was now Roz's duty to defeat the king. He had to keep his brother's promise—even if it brought them together again.